Day Of The Damned

By
Des Dunn

as
Sheldon B. Cole

First Published by Cleveland Publishing.

Republished in 2026 by Echo Books.

Echo Books is an imprint of Superscript Publishing Pty Ltd.
ABN 76 644 812 395.

Registered Office: 35 Keeley Lane, Princes Hill, Victoria, 3054.
www.echobooks.com.au

Book Design: Jason McGregor.

ISBN: 978-1-923441-33-0 (Paperback)
ISBN: 978-1-922603-64-7 (ePub)

CHAPTER ONE
West of Everything

It was mid-afternoon when the rain stopped and Blake Durant drew rein on Sundown, his blue-black stallion, on the crest of a lonely, wind-swept hill. The rain-washed air was so clear that he had no difficulty making out the town a mile or so in the distance. It was a welcome sight after the past week's trail-blazing across desolate distances, and Durant felt a new lease of life surging through him.

From where he had drawn up on the sagebrush-studded crest, the town of Maple looked smaller than he had been led to expect it to be. Despite the wide streets and some double-storied buildings, it was mostly just a cluster of rundown houses and stores thrown together haphazardly on the prairie, with cattle yards at the end of one street towards the west, and two adobe huts standing opposite each other at the eastern end to form a kind of gateway.

There was little activity in the streets, but Blake put this down to the fact that the town had probably been as badly buffeted by the day's storms as he had. He pulled his range coat tighter about his wide-shouldered body and, giving Sundown his head, let the horse pick its own way down the hillside and across the prairie where rain still lay in puddles.

Sundown was into a canter by the time they reached the edge of town and as Durant rode into the main street he pulled the horse down to a walk and let his gaze sweep the place.

A bunch of cowhands brushing rain off their shoulders were dismounting from tired-looking range ponies outside a batwinged doorway. Most of them looked Durant over, then disregarded him, apparently accepting him as one of their kind who had come out of the range and was in need of a drink and a feed and some rest.

Blake rode the stallion to the rack and dropped to the ground. He hitched the horse and stood a moment letting the sensation of weight shift down his legs. The cramp in his limbs slowly dissolved as he opened his coat, gave Sundown a pat on the head and moved towards the batwings.

The bunch of cowboys had already gone on into the saloon and when Blake drew up at the counter, he saw them grouped at the end of the room, talking with the barkeeper. Blake waited for the barkeeper to serve the cowhands before he indicated with a gesture that he wanted a drink. The barkeeper, a barrel-chested, sullen looking man, eyed him coolly, picked up a bottle and a glass in one hand. After giving the counter between Blake and himself a wipe with his sleeve, he put the glass down and filled it. He mumbled the price and moved away after Blake paid him.

Blake leaned his tall, rangy body against the counter and stared somberly into his drink, letting his thoughts drift to other times and other places.

Maple was in the mid-west on the direct trail to his own home and he wondered if it was time he headed that way, to see how things were going, and how his brother was coping with the ranch. There were a few people he would like to see again, but only a few.

Maybe, he told himself, as he often did, that if he saw again the country he and Louise had ridden over, it would erase his painful sense of loss and wipe away the memories he had drifted to forget. Perhaps time had done its work, and he could once again pick up the threads of a life he had forsaken for the loneliness of strange places and stranger people.

Perhaps... he could never be sure.

A hoarse voice broke into his distant thoughts.

"Something wrong with the whisky, stranger?"

Blake looked up from the drink and saw the barkeeper holding a bottle tipped towards the rim of his glass.

Blake shook his head. "No."

"You havin' a refill then?" the man muttered. "I ain't got the time to keep comin' up this way, mister. You fill up now or wait till I'm ready next time."

Blake shrugged, then tossed the drink down and slid some more money forward. The barkeeper smiled in a self-satisfied manner as he poured the drink, then, looking pleased with himself, went off.

Blake heard talk rising about him, but none of it interested him. His mind went back a month to when he had left the Damiani ranch and the picture of Len Damiani was as clear now as it was then, the old man crippled with arthritis, standing at the head of his wife's grave, the winter closing in fast.

He remembered, too, a pretty schoolteacher who had paid frequent visits to the ranch during his stay there. He had wanted to say goodbye to her, but had not. He knew he had in a way taken the coward's way out, preferring to ride off rather than test his own feelings towards her. They had enjoyed each other's company and perhaps, if he had given their friendship a chance, it might have turned out to be something deeper and more rewarding. Perhaps...

The barkeeper was back again with the bottle poised. Blake finished his second drink and pushed more change forward. The man muttered something under his breath and was on the point of moving away when Blake asked him, "You know a man named Danny Damiani?"

The barkeeper stopped on the spot and swung back, brow creased into a frown. "Yeah, I know Damiani."

"He about?"

The man looked uneasily down the counter. Blake noticed that the cowhands had stopped talking.

"Ain't in yet," the barkeeper said. "But he will be. You... you a friend of his?"

"Nope."

The barkeeper's self-assurance seemed to have deserted him. He licked his lips and wiped a grubby hand down his shirt front, leaving a wide sweat stain on it.

Then he nodded towards the cowhands. "They ride with Danny. Maybe they can help you more'n I can."

Blake looked disinterestedly at the bunch. "No, it's private business."

The barkeeper studied Blake more intently and his sudden increase in nervousness seemed to indicate that in Blake Durant he saw a man he would do better not knowing. Blake ignored his probing look and went back to his drinking. But he had only got halfway through his third drink when heavy footsteps sounded on his left. He did not look up even when the smell of stale whisky and tobacco reached across to him.

"Looks like you come a ways in a hurry, stranger," a voice said a moment later.

Blake looked sideways to find a big, heavily built cowhand standing there. The man wore no hat and thick red hair fell in heavy curls down his creased brow. His eyes were clear blue and cold in their appraisal of Durant.

"I came a ways, yes," Blake told him. "But not in a hurry."

The redhead straightened, brow tightening into a deeper frown. Then he brushed past Blake and walked to the batwings. He took a moment studying Sundown before he came back nodding his head as if he had suddenly decided something for himself.

"The black's not been pushed," he said.

"I told you that."

The redhead's lips drew back over his teeth. He could have been smiling, except that his eyes stayed as cold as the winter wind. He was a massively built man, yet when he had walked to the door he had shown himself light on his feet. His face was marked a little but not much, which Blake took as a sign that he could possibly look after himself, and liked to test himself out from time to time.

"Yeah, you told me that, stranger," he said finally. "Now tell me your name and what you want with Danny."

Blake straightened, put down his glass. He noticed a closer bunching of the other cowhands. The only other men in the bar were a knot of businessmen right down the far end. They seemed to want no part of this discussion, and in fact seemed to be showing a deep interest in their drinks.

"You know Damiani?" Blake asked.

The redhead's face darkened under a rise of anger. "Yeah, Danny's a friend of mine, mister. Now out with your name and where'd you come from and why."

Blake allowed a smile to touch the corners of his mouth. Len Damiani had told him that his son, Danny, was a wild one. So Blake knew that this was a wild bunch. But he remained unworried, mainly because he didn't expect to have to tangle with them to any real degree.

"For what it's worth, mister," he said, "the name is Blake Durant. Where I come from is none of your business and what I want with Damiani is none of your business, either. Your friends are waiting for you."

The redhead straightened fully upright now and his fists came together at his gun belt buckle. His face was a mottled patchwork of angry red and livid white and there were lines of tension at the corners of his mouth.

"Durant, eh," he growled. "Maybe you're on the hunt, eh?"

"Nope."

"Damn you, you ain't the first and you likely won't be the last! But, by hell, if you got a mind to come hunting a man, you say it straight and we'll get to the core of it real quick, here and now."

"What do they call you, mister?" Blake asked him calmly.

"Name's Bromage... Curly Bromage." Bromage's shoulders went back and he planted his feet wide, as if in defiance of what else Blake might say to him.

"Okay, now we know each other, Bromage," Blake said flatly. "For what it's worth, that's as far as I want our association to go. I rode in to have a talk to Damiani if he was about. There's no more to it and I don't want anybody reading any more into it than that. Got it?"

Bromage looked slightly unsure of himself, but before he could make any reply, the batwings creaked. Bromage's look swung to the doorway and his anger seemed to soften a little.

Blake turned slightly to find a tall, lean man in carefully tailored clothes standing in the doorway. A gold watch chain decorated his sky blue vest. He wore no hat and no gun belt.

"Bromage, you and the boys ready?" said the man. "We're ready to start. Damiani's outside waiting."

Blake finished his drink as the cowhands clattered their glasses on the counter. When they came up to Curly Bromage, the big man growled, "Well, Durant, here's your chance. Come meet Danny."

"Sure," Blake said. He put down his glass, eyed the bunch of cowhands casually and led the way to the batwings. The tall, lean man stepped out onto the boardwalk and Blake followed him to see two wagons in the street with horses hitched behind, two drivers already up, and three riders circling at the front of the lead wagon.

It was immediately plain to Blake that Danny Damiani, whichever one he was, was on the way out of town. Not wanting to let him go without passing on Len Damiani's information, Blake called, "Which one of you is Damiani?"

Even as Blake spoke, Curly Bromage came hurrying out through the batwings and called out, "Danny, stranger name of Durant just came a long way to see you. Actin' just like them others."

Blake saw a dark-haired, good-looking young man step out from behind the second of the two wagons. His black eyes swept up and down Blake and his mouth curled in a sneer.

"That so, Durant?" he said. "Where from? Who sent you?"

Bromage and the other cowhands had quickly formed a circle off from Blake Durant. Blake scowled at Bromage who gave him a crooked grin.

Danny Damiani quickly gestured with his left hand and said, "Easy now, Curly. I can handle this. Let Durant have his say."

Blake looked from one to the other, seeing the arrogance and conceit in Damiani's eyes. The youngster's sneer had switched to a smile and he looked very cool and assured, though Blake noted that the fingers of his right hand curled very close to his gun butt.

"From the Platte, Damiani," said Blake, "with word from your father."

Damiani's self-assurance vanished. His dark eyes took on a brooding depth and his mouth curled again into a sneer, ruining the regular handsomeness of his features, showing the mean temper locked inside him.

"Pa?" he asked. "What does he want with me?"

"I've a message for you," said Blake. "It's private enough for me to tell you on your own."

When Damiani just stood there in silence, frowning, Curly Bromage called, "Don't take his word for that, Danny. Hell, he likely ain't dumb enough that he can't see the way things stand here. But on your own, he could trick you."

"Shut down, Curly," was Damiani's quick response to that. Then he nodded at Blake, adding, "Get it out, Durant."

Blake pulled his rain-dampened bandanna from about his neck and shrugged. "Okay, Damiani, if that's the way you want it. Your ma's dead. I guess, at that, there's no way to make it sound any easier."

The color drained from Danny Damiani's face and his mouth opened and a pained groan came from him. But then he was quickly in control of his emotions again. He bit his bottom lip and waved towards the wagons. "Get the boys up, Curly," he said in a strained voice. "Everything's settled." He then came across to Blake, eyeing him intently. His lips were trembling as if he was trying to get some control into his thoughts.

"It's the truth?" he asked Blake.

"Sure. I worked for your father for three months. Your mother died during my stay there."

"What from, Durant?"

Blake was not sure if there were tears in Damiani's eyes, or whether the gleam was caused by a trick of the late afternoon light after the storm.

"Natural causes," said Blake. "She went to sleep and didn't wake up. Your pa buried her on the place, behind the house. I stayed on another month but with the winter closing in, headed on my way. Your pa asked me if I came up this way to look you up, and tell you to come on home."

Damiani straightened, his face suddenly twisted with rage. "Come home?" he barked. "What in hell to? My old man hasn't ever been anything to me. The stinkin', mean-bellied polecat, half-starvin' ma all the time—"

Blake cut him off, saying curtly, "I've brought you the message."

He was turning away when Damiani grabbed his shoulder and roughly wheeled him back. "Damn you, Durant, I'm telling you that—"

"It's no business of mine, Damiani," said Blake. He prised the young gun hand's fingers open and stepped back.

But Danny Damiani yelled, "My pa is a saddlebum, Durant. He never done nothin' in his whole life for anybody but himself. From the time I was ten years old he had me workin' from sunup till sundown, and for no reward apart from enough grub to keep me fit enough to work. Go home! He'd have to be loco to expect that."

Blake had begun to walk away. The other hands who had been with Bromage in the saloon had already grouped about the back of the wagons, and the three riders were sitting their horses, watching them very closely. In fact so closely that Blake thought they looked more like guards than men paid to play escort to a wagon train moving out.

Then, as Damiani's shouting died away and he began to curse, a rider came charging into town. Blake looked round to see an old man, with a mane of white hair flowing down to his shoulders, and a thick white beard covering the whole bottom part of his face, charging down on them.

The old man had a rifle flattened against the side of his horse and as soon as he cleared the front of the first wagon, he sent his horse racing towards the well-dressed man still waiting on the boardwalk outside the saloon.

Blake turned, aware that tension flickered along the whole length of the street, like the feeling of thunder in the air before a storm. And then the tension climaxed in a booming roll of gunfire as the old man released his grip on the reins and brought the rifle to his shoulder. He pumped off two wild shots which tore into the saloon batwings. By then the well-dressed man had sought the cover of an overhang post and the three riders had closed in, guns barking.

Caught in the middle of all this, Blake Durant threw himself sideways and rolled out of the vicious crossfire. Sundown, on a loose tie-rope at the hitchrack, reared and pawed the air with his front legs as bullets whipped about him. Then the old man let out a scream of pain just as his horse slammed into Sundown. In the wild melee that followed, Sundown and the old-timer's horse went down in a tangle of kicking legs.

The old man was thrown clear of both horses. He landed on his back on the boardwalk and rolled onto his side, still clutching the rifle. As he did so more bullets slammed into him, punching him over onto his knees.

A further bullet missed him and smashed into his rifle stock, knocking the weapon from his grasp. He rocked back on his haunches and sat there, blood streaming down the side of his face and filling the folds of his grubby shirt. Then he fell forward onto his knees again, cursing wildly, and finally pointing a grubby hand at the well-dressed man.

"Damn you, Berry," he cried hoarsely, "you're a liar, and a cheat and a thief! You ain't got nothin' out there for any decent man to want. And you ain't payin' in nothin' but bullets for the work done. By hell—"

The old man's words were cut off as another blast of gunfire ripped into him and he fell back, dead. Blake came slowly to his feet, watching the man called Berry very closely. He saw the anger rise in his face, mixed with uncertainty, and then he heeled about, and shouted, "Gilbert, Hopgood, get them in! I want all their guns left out and see nobody pulls out on me."

Danny Damiani, standing with a confused Curly Bromage, was the first to react to this order. His hand went down towards his gun, but before he could clear leather one of the riders bore down on him and sent him flying against the back of the wagon.

Curly Bromage threw himself at the rider but was knocked aside by a swinging gun butt which caught him on the side of the jaw. The others from the saloon were all trying to get space enough to fight in but they were suddenly hemmed in by the three horsemen and the guns that were lowered to cover them.

Berry came off the boardwalk after stepping over the old man's body. None of the saloon drinkers had come out and only the barkeeper's worried face showed to Blake's glance as he checked out the saloon. Then Berry had a gun in his back and said, "You, too, Durant. Get into one of them wagons."

"I'm not part of this crowd," Blake told him. "I'm on the drift."

"Get in, damn you!" Berry shouted angrily and pushed Blake roughly forward.

Blake went only a pace forward with the push and swung about, his left hand sweeping in a circle to catch hold of Berry's wrist. Berry swore violently and tried to wrestle his hand free, but Blake pulled him closer and slammed a fist into his stomach. When Berry doubled over, Blake turned him about and drove his gun-loaded hand up his back. He had almost prised Berry's fist open when a horse crashed into him and threw him sideways.

Before he could regain his balance, a big man hurled himself out of the saddle and he was smashed to the ground by the weight of the man's body.

Blake felt the breath crushed from his lungs by the impact and then a gun butt came down onto the side of his head. He felt blood run as the pain exploded behind his eyes. Then the daylight was gone and all sound stopped.

Watching from the corner of one of the wagons and wiping blood from his mouth, Danny Damiani gave a grunt and elbowed Curly Bromage out of his way. His companions stood there, gun belts at their feet. Damiani's vicious stare slashed over them and his lips peeled back in a snarl of defiance as he turned back to face Berry.

"By hell, Berry," he said tightly, "what the blazes do you think you're doing? You can't handle this bunch. By hell, we'll tear you and those scum of yours to pieces."

"Silence him!" came the order from Berry.

Before Damiani could turn, a gun butt put paid to him from behind. Curly Bromage, still looking dazed, picked him up and pushed his unconscious body into the wagon and then he and the other hands from the saloon were herded into the wagon.

Berry had Blake Durant picked up and thrown into the other wagon and then had Durant's big black stallion caught and tied to the rear of the wagon. Going to his own horse, Berry gave the order to move out, and the Maple townspeople, who until this time had stayed behind cover, now began to come hesitantly into the street.

The barkeeper was among them, standing taller than anybody else. He said gruffly, "Glad to see the last of that wild bunch. By hell, this town can do without the whole shebang of them."

Nobody answered him as the two wagons with their accompanying riders ranged on each side, headed out of Maple, taking a course directly towards the west.

CHAPTER TWO
The Stockade

Torp Berry mopped his brow where a heavy film of sweat had formed, despite the coolness of the night.

"Bundle 'em in!" he shouted. "No beg-pardons. Just put 'em away and get those gates closed!"

He kept moving about across the front of the high-walled compound, his gun always shifting, covering the movements of everybody about him. Lantern light showed his features drawn and pinched, his eyes warily searching, as if, even with everything seemingly under control, he suspected that a change for the worse might come if he let it.

Bart Gilbert, a lean man with a scarred cheek and a permanent limp, stood by the gate of the compound, rifle lifted, ready to shoot down any of the cowhands who gave trouble.

Near the two drawn-up wagons Will Hopgood prodded and pushed and dragged the men, until he had all of them inside the walls. Then he backed off, closed the gate and put three lengths of timber in place across it. Then he took hold of the gate and tried to shake it. When it did not move an inch, despite his immense strength, he breathed a sigh of satisfaction. "All fixed, Torp," he said.

"Fine," said Berry. "Stand two guards right through the night. This is the wildest bunch we've had and I don't want them given any quarter at all, you hear. And no rations until I'm satisfied they've seen who's boss here."

"I'd like me a slice of Damiani, Torp," Will Hopgood said as he wiped the sweat from his broad, heavily lined brow. He moved away from the stockade gate with a stamping, bow-legged gait that pounded sound into the sunbaked mud of the clearing.

Torp Berry left Hopgood to place the guards and went off with Bart Gilbert across to the main ranch house. A hundred yards away, it stood solid and seemingly indestructible under the pale wash of the night's moonlight. There was a guard on duty at either end of the long verandah. The roof was slanted upwards with a parapet running its front length in which foot-wide holes had been cut to allow up to fifty men to lie flat and overlook the clearing itself. Torp Berry's stare lifted to those fortress-like openings and he rubbed his jaw thoughtfully.

He went up onto the porch and stood at the rail, with Gilbert alongside him. A few minutes later Will Hopgood joined them. Hopgood pulled himself up onto the rail and let his bowed legs swing, his bootheels continually drumming out sound on the palings.

Berry eyed him intently for some time before he said, "Will, this is not only the wildest bunch we've had, but the biggest and the toughest. They're just what we want to get all the timber we need and then cut through that mountain. But, by hell, you've got to keep your eye on Damiani. If we can tame him we can tame the rest."

"Except Durant," Will Hopgood told him. "From what I heard he isn't part of this bunch. And he's tough, fast, and hard."

Berry's gaze went flint-hard. "I'll handle Durant if he steps out of line, Will. I got a score to settle with that drifter that I ain't going to forget. But what we've all got to keep in mind, is that we need men strong enough to get up that mountain. We got to feed them enough to keep their strength up but at the same time keep them trimmed down so they can't fight back. With the others we've had here, it's been easy, because their spirits broke in a couple of days. This bunch is going to take longer, but I don't want it too much longer. We got to get through the hill before the rains set in. If we don't, we'll have a half year to wait."

"They'll work," Will Hopgood assured Berry and, grinning evilly, went on, "Or by hell, I'll flog them till they can't stand up." He turned to Gilbert, said, "Bart, you stick close to me at all times. If some of them get loco ideas I don't want them shot down. Just nicked maybe to keep them in line. My whip will do the rest."

Hopgood pushed himself to his feet, eyed the guards outside the stockade gate and then looked questioningly at Torp Berry.

"Time for a little celebration, Torp, eh?" he said smilingly. "The men earned that today. Not a thing went wrong."

Torp Berry frowned and hesitated for a moment before he nodded agreement to the suggestion. "Okay, but keep away from the Soncum girl, Will," he said sharply.

Will Hopgood looked disappointed. "But hell, Torp, you said, after you'd finished with her, I could."

"Well, I'm not finished with her yet," Berry cut in. "And I don't want her to know her father didn't make it. Tomorrow, we'll question the men left behind and see how in blazes Soncum got away in the first place. I want to know the name of the man who was responsible. Right?"

"Okay," Hopgood muttered, hiding his scowl behind a hand that rubbed at his stubbled jaw. He stayed silent, still scowling, until Torp Berry went off into the house. Then, with a sullen look towards a second ranch house standing forty yards up the clearing near the barn, he growled to Gilbert, "Get Al and Joe, and four bottles. Might as well pick up them saloon tramps as you come. Guess we could do worse."

"I get a chance at Bess?" Gilbert asked eagerly. Hopgood studied him bleakly for a moment before he snapped, "What the hell you want with that old bag, Bart? Hell, the stink of her is enough to turn a man off his drink."

"Don't smell to me," Bart Gilbert said. "Don't reckon I want it spoken about her like that either, Will. Hell, I waited my turn long enough, ain't I? I done everything you wanted this far."

Hopgood grunted something under his breath and stepped off the porch. He looked back into the house where he could see Torp Berry talking quietly to somebody inside who was cut off from his view by the heavy window drapes. He knew the Soncum girl was in there. He ran his tongue over suddenly dry lips as he pictured her, full-bodied and young, as pretty as any woman he had ever seen in his life before. He ran a hand over his face, and his eyes narrowed at the thought of getting his hands on her. Hell, he wanted her bad, he thought fiercely, and he meant one day to have her, and to hell with Berry and all his slow going.

Hopgood moved up the clearing towards the second, smaller ranch house and watched Bart Gilbert go off at a run to fetch two of the other hired guns and the four saloon women they had brought with them from their last visit to Lusc.

Hopgood thought about each of the women in turn but always, despite their availability, and the fact that as ramrod he had first choice of them, his mind continually went back to the picture May Soncum had made getting out of her father's rig, with her skirt high and all that smooth white flesh showing and her bosom threatening to burst right out of her thin cotton blouse. By hell, he told himself, one day, and soon, he was going to see what else she was made of.

He climbed up to the verandah of the smaller ranch house and, after unlocking the door, called out to the women inside, "Okay, we're going to have a party. Get the place cleaned up and rustle up some grub. It's Bart, Al, Joe and me and you better enjoy it, or look like you do because we had us a real hard day in town."

Hopgood didn't wait for an answer, but turned about and crossed back to the porch rail. He thought of the first time he had met Torp Berry when Berry was a small town lawman down Santos way, bleeding the town dry and getting out just ahead of a lynch mob. That was three years ago and in their travels together, Berry had emerged as boss man with Will Hopgood as his top hand. Will hadn't minded that until now, but tonight the thought of May Soncum put rebellion into his heart.

He tried to shake the feeling off, remembering how strong Berry was with the rest of the men, giving them a better life than any of them could possibly get elsewhere, with plenty of good food, easy women, some action now and then, and the promise of untold wealth for every man when they completed their work on the mountain.

He was still there brooding to himself when Bart
Gilbert, still on the run and carrying four bottles, came
across the clearing. Will Hopgood turned into the house
and prepared himself for as good a night as he could
expect with the company at his disposal.

* * *

Blake Durant lay on the hard ground and watched
the clouds shift across the face of the pale moon. His
head ached and the blood had dried on the cut on
his forehead, making it feel as if a sawbones had put
stitches in it. But he was sure that no sawbones had
visited this hell hole that evening. Nor did he think, on
putting two and two together, that a sawbones was ever
likely to visit.

Rising on one elbow when he heard sound on his
right, he peered through the gloom to find Damiani and
Curly Bromage coming towards him. Damiani looked
ready to tear the stockade wall to pieces with his
bare hands. He drew up alongside Durant and after a
moment's disdainful study of Blake, he went down on
his haunches, picked up a stick and began scratching in
the dirt with it.

"What we've found out, Durant," he said quietly, "is
that we're prisoners here. Seems we ain't the first,
either, who have been carted out and held here."

Damiani continued, "two derelicts back along the far wall have been here four months and are no more'n skin and bone and won't even talk against Berry and Hopgood. They ain't got a single inch of their backs which hasn't been whipped raw one time or another and the stink of them would turn a buffalo skinner's stomach."

Blake eased himself into a sitting position. Despite the knock on the forehead, he felt himself to be in pretty good shape, though still a little cramped in the limbs.

"So, Damiani?" he asked.

Damiani dug the stick viciously into the ground and gouged out a lump of clay. He glanced at Curly Bromage who was sitting off to one side and said, "So we ain't stayin' about until we get like them old fools. What we know is there's only two guards on duty and there's eleven of us. We just held a meeting and we figure we can knock that wall down if we all charge it." He brought his fist down on the lump of clay he'd dug out of the ground and squashed it flat. "It'll go down easy as that."

Blake looked at the wall and shook his head. "It's made of adobe reinforced with stakes and I reckon it's wired, too. It'd hold against a battering ram with all our weight behind it."

Damiani glared furiously at him, snapped, "Well, we're going to try, damn you! You buying in or staying out?"

Blake pursed his lips and shook his head. "I don't think it can work, Damiani. In fact, I think it would be loco. Some of your men will get killed."

"To hell with you," snarled Damiani as he pushed himself to his feet. He stood there still glaring furiously at Blake Durant, then he went on in a rush of words, "I'm obliged for the message about my ma, Durant. But that's all I'm obliged to you for. From what I seen back there in town, you ain't worth a spit in a fight. You had a chance and missed it."

Blake did not argue with him nor did he bother to remind Damiani that if anybody had been made a fool of in Maple, it was Damiani himself.

"Good luck," Blake drawled and Curly Bromage took a step towards him, his other foot going back in preparation for a kick. But Damiani pushed him away, saying, "Come on, Curly, we don't need him. First through that wall will have the best chance. Those left behind will sure enough be made pay for the others getting away."

Damiani turned and drew Curly Bromage back with him. The dark had just swallowed them when a high-pitched squeal of laughter came from outside the stockade wall.

Blake heard the footsteps stop, then Bromage say in a surprised tone, "Hell, they got womenfolk out there."

"And drink," Damiani put back. "Which suits me right fine. We'll give Berry and his jackals an hour to get themselves boozed up, then make our move. Come on."

They went off, leaving Blake Durant to listen for the next hour to laughter that became more and more raucous, punctuated by bottles smashing, now and then some shots being fired off, and bursts of bawdy singing.

He could also hear the guards doing their rounds of the stockade wall, meeting just by the gate and then turning back on their sentry walk. He rose and brushed down his clothes. The air was cool and he felt a chill beginning to penetrate his clothing. That in itself told him he was in high country, possibly a long way from the plains. But how far from Maple he did not know.

Then he heard somebody call drunkenly, "Will, get over here."

It was only about a minute later that a young woman's voice cried out through the night, "No, for God's sake, no!"

"It's him or me," a man said roughly. "Take your pick, damn you! I ain't puttin' up with no more of your damned sass."

Blake heard the sound of a slap, a muffled cry, then sobbing from not far away. He rose to his feet and went towards the stockade wall. But although he searched along it for several minutes he could find no hole to peer through to see what was going on.

Then a man's gruff voice said, "Bart, you and the others clear outa here. Take those other damn women with you, too, and keep them quiet. I'm havin' me some comfort tonight for once."

There was another long time of silence before Blake heard a door slammed shut. Then another scream broke the night's stillness. He felt a chill run down his spine. A second scream came and then a third, followed by muffled groans and finally a deathlike stillness.

Behind him he heard Danny Damiani call out, "Now! Full go, and no stopping!"

The pounding of many feet sounded across the stockade clearing before a solid mass of bodies crashed into the gate. The gate shook a little but did not look like giving. Then Blake heard the guards running back towards the gateway.

He yelled out, "Get down, you fools! They'll cut you to pieces!"

Even as he spoke, two rifles opened up and a volley of bullets tore through the gate. Blake heard one of Damiani's men howl in pain. Four others hit the ground and lay outstretched, unmoving. Damiani summoned the others to him and they flattened themselves against the wall just off from the gate. They were conferring in urgent whispers, when a voice called, "You in there, try that again and we'll drag a couple of you out for flogging. Back now and behave."

"Now!" Damiani called again and seven men charged at the gate, this time two of them forming a stepping stone for Curly Bromage to climb onto and reach out for the top. But just as Bromage's fingers took hold and he began to draw himself up, lantern light found him.

Blake heard the guards stepping back just before a vicious blast of gunfire sprayed the top of the wall and Bromage dropped down again, groaning in pain. Danny Damiani grabbed him and pulled him off to the side as another blast of gunfire tore through the gate.

Then a savage voice said, "Get lights and then get that gate open!"

Danny Damiani collected his men and came hurrying through the shadows to stop just short of Blake Durant. His crazy stare sought out Blake and he hissed a curse. Blake had the impression that Damiani would have liked to go further than that, but right then the gate opened and a stream of men came through it carrying lanterns. At the rear of the visiting bunch was the big man Blake had seen in town and who did everything Berry had asked of him with a ruthlessness that Blake had not forgotten.

Will Hopgood pushed his way to the front of his men and flicked a whip out, back and forth across the compound floor.

When he saw the group huddled against the far wall, a smile broke across his mouth. "Bart, get a couple of them and string them up," he growled. "Then bunch the others so they can watch."

Blake rose to his feet and stood at the back of the suddenly shifting crowd of Damiani followers. A lean man, holding a rifle and using it to clear his way through the crowd, came forward and prodded Curly Bromage out of the pack. Then he shepherded a man named Warlow after him. Damiani stepped forward, cursing, and tried to get at Bart Gilbert's gun. Hopgood stepped up, took him by the shoulder and wheeled him after Bromage and Warlow.

Hopgood positioned his guards to watch Blake Durant and the others and then supervised the tying up of his three prisoners.

Blake Durant watched Danny Damiani only. It was plain to Damiani as it was to the others what was in store for them, but Damiani's face showed no sign of fear, and rebellion still rode high through his defiant stare. "You're yeller, Hopgood," he muttered fiercely. "You want a fight, why not you and me, two out?"

Hopgood's answer was to bring the lash of the whip across Damiani's face. Damiani went back on his heels, straining to free his tied hands. Grinning evilly, Hopgood walked behind the three of them and put two lashes across each of the men's backs. Then he stood swinging the whip back and forth and announced, "Gents, that was just a warm up. Now, maybe it was my fault before for not telling you that you're here to stay, and there ain't no way out. So you can either work for your keep and stay out of trouble or you can do it the hard way. But think on this... the next time you get a loco idea about making trouble, you remember what's happened tonight."

Hopgood moved into the wash of the moonlight and Blake saw deep nail marks down both of his cheeks. He remembered the screams of the young woman and knew with absolute certainty that she had inflicted those marks on Hopgood. But what he had done to her afterwards he did not want to think about.

So he stood and listened to the slash of the whip and the grunts of Damiani and Curly Bromage. Warlow began to whimper and then to beg and Hopgood gave him three more vicious cuts before Warlow sagged and Hopgood told Gilbert to cut him down.

Damiani turned against the strain of his ropes and spat into Hopgood's face. In a wild fury, Hopgood began beating him brutally until Danny Damiani's body began to sag, but no sound came out of him.

Watching this, Curly Bromage said, "Hopgood, if I get outa this, I'm goin' to kill you. I'll kill you sure."

"You ain't goin' no place, big man," Hopgood shouted, his voice thick with venom. "None of you is going any place because there isn't any place to go. Back of you there's a fifty mile desert and in front of you the mountains. You ain't got no water and no grub and no horses, and by the time I'm finished with you in two days' time there ain't any of you going to be fit for anything but lying on the ground and begging for mercy."

Hopgood stood back, wiped his face with his sleeve and belted into Curly Bromage with renewed enthusiasm until Bromage's body sagged and he fell to be held up by his tied wrists. Hopgood told Gilbert to cut him and Damiani down, then walked across to the others. His gaze sought out Blake Durant and he pointed the whip handle at him and said, "You, mister, you're first in the morning. Come sunup I'll be coming back. So all night you just sit and think about it. Damiani showed he ain't all that tough when it comes to mixing with me, and every damn one of you is going to find out the same. What you got to do, to save yourself some trouble," he went on, "is call for one of the guards, any time of the day or night, and agree to work for Torp Berry and me. That way you'll get grub, water and will be separated and protected from the fools left in there to boil up through the day and freeze during the night and die of thirst during both."

Laughing scornfully then, Will Hopgood walked off and the guards, evidently working to a pattern, formed a line between him and the prisoners and began backing towards the gates.

When the gates closed, Blake Durant was the first to Danny Damiani. He picked him up from the ground and carried him over into the moonlight and turned him onto his stomach. He then removed his torn and bloodied shirt and sucked in a quick breath when he saw the torn flesh. He was wondering how long it would take for infection to set in when a cloth-wrapped bundle came flying over the wall to land a short distance away from him.

Then Hopgood's voice said, "Durant, you bein' the next one in line, you get to teachin' them others what to do. You rub in the salt and dry up the blood, then you paste the lard over the gashes. That way you don't die, not right away anyway."

Hopgood's mocking laugh was loud in the night as the men gathered about Damiani, Warlow and Bromage. Blake looked at each man in turn, then muttered, "It'll be the best thing to do anyway."

With that he walked away, leaving Danny Damiani to be tended by his own men, as he knew Damiani would wish.

CHAPTER THREE
The Girl

Torp Berry stood in the open gateway of the stockade with four armed men behind him. He was clean-shaven, tidily dressed, and studied the line of prisoners with an easy, almost nonchalant, look. Blake Durant met his eyes and their stares locked for a moment but neither man spoke.

Will Hopgood and Bart Gilbert were positioned just inside the wall. Hopgood carried the short whip with which he had lashed Warlow, Damiani and Bromage the previous evening. Gilbert looked uneasy but Hopgood's face was wreathed in a smile although the scratches of the previous night's incident with the young woman still showed clearly.

Torp Berry stepped forward and said briskly, "Men, I hope you slept well last night. From what I saw of you yesterday, you are a hardy bunch and used to sleeping on the ground under the stars. That's fine, because all the time you are here working for me, you will be doing just that. No matter, I don't intend to make your stay any more uncomfortable than that unless you force me to change things."

Berry came closer to the men and smiled widely before pointing at the stockade walls. "You will see that at regular intervals along the wall, my men have put in iron rings."

Berry continued, "every night when you come back from working on the mountain I want each of you to go to a ring and stand there until Will and Bart come with your chains. After a meal, which you will find equal to the work you have done that day, each of you will be chained to a ring until morning. I hate to do this to men like you but you will understand that I have no choice after last night's attempt to escape. Also, you must understand that I cannot allow any talk at night, which would enable plans to be made and things like that. There will be absolute silence from the time you walk in here. You hear me?"

Not a man spoke. Blake Durant threw a glance at Damiani and found him scowling as fiercely as ever. Curly Bromage, however, looked a little more subdued this morning than he had been the previous evening. He stood with his hands inside his shirt and Blake could see bloodstains all over the faded cloth. Berry seemed unconcerned at the lack of response. He began to walk up and down in front of the prisoners' line, again taking stock of each man. When he reached Danny Damiani he grabbed his shoulder and wheeled him around. Damiani's tattered shirt covered very little of his slashed back.

Berry inspected his wounds and, smiling thinly, said, "Pity about that, Damiani. But I hope you've learned your lesson. There is no way out of here and we have no visitors in this isolated section. As soon as I leave here you will be given rations and some water to drink and wash up in."

Berry continued, "I want you to convince them that it is common sense to work and work hard. You, in particular, will be treated according to the work your men do."

Damiani lifted his head and glared furiously back at Torp Berry. Berry smiled tolerantly and shrugged his lean shoulders. He went on down the line, stopped in front of Curly Bromage.

"Same goes for you, Bromage," he said. "I know a great deal about you, because I made it my business to check you men out thoroughly while you were helling it up in Maple. I know how strong you are and how stubborn and how loyal to Damiani you are. So you go along with Damiani and get me all the work done I want done each day."

Curly Bromage's lips curled slightly and for a moment Blake Durant feared that the big man was going to lunge at Berry. But Berry went on, inspected the rest of the men, and then crossed back to Will Hopgood's side.

"Full rations, Will," he said loudly, "until we see how sensible they're going to be."

Berry turned and was walking out of the stockade when an explosion sounded off in the distance. All the men turned and stared in the direction of the sound. A second explosion disturbed the morning's silence, then Berry, looking very pleased with himself, went on out of the stockade.

Hopgood made a gesture and four men carried a bucket and tin plates into the stockade. They set them down before the line of prisoners and made a hasty retreat outside the wall again. One man returned with a bucket of water and a tin mug and again retreated quickly, covered by the menacing rifles of his fellow guards.

Hopgood indicated the food and water with his whip and said, "Help yourselves. You've got fifteen minutes and then we go for a walk. All of us, and that includes those whipped last night. There'll be no shirkers in this camp, I promise you."

With that, Hopgood, Gilbert and the other guards backed off, the guards keeping their guns trained on the line of men. When the gate closed and the big bearers were pushed home, Blake Durant moved out of the line. There was a sudden rush for the food and water and when Danny Damiani and Curly Bromage did not try to stop the rush, Blake snapped, "Hold it now, all of you!"

The authority in Blake's voice stopped the men in their tracks. Their looks swung back to him and confusion showed in each face. Then Danny Damiani worked his way to the front of the men and growled, "Hold it for what, Durant? So you can have first go at the grub?"

Blake shook his head. "In a rush more food will be spilled than consumed, and by the look of it there isn't enough to go round as it is. I think we should appoint somebody to take charge of the distribution."

Damiani gaped at him and then snarled, "You, maybe?"

Blake shook his head. "Nope. I'm the outsider here, except that while we're here I'm one of you, caught up in the same miserable business. But where food and drink are concerned we've got to see everybody gets his share. That means the older men and the smaller men equally with the young and the powerful."

Blake felt Curly Bromage's look fixed on him. He looked at the others and finally saw Warlow standing with shoulders hunched and face lined with pain.

"Why not Warlow?" he asked them all. "He's been beaten badly so I doubt if anybody here will want to argue with his distribution. Also he's about the oldest here and from what I've seen has the respect of most of you men."

Damiani turned and scowled questioningly at the other prisoners. Josh Warlow lifted his head and frowned heavily across at Durant.

When nobody voiced disagreement with Durant, Warlow muttered, "Durant's talkin' sense and you men can trust me. We got to scrape the bottom of the barrel on this one and can't afford no spills. Line up and leave the rest to me." Danny Damiani still looked doubtfully at Blake Durant, but before he could promote further argument, Curly Bromage pushed some of the men forward and took his place fifth in line.

Quickly the others formed up and when Warlow began serving out the food, Damiani moved to where Blake Durant had gone to the end of the line.

Leering, Damiani said, "Smart, Durant, real smart."

"Just sensible, Damiani," Blake told him.

"Yeah, I'll grant that, big man," Damiani said. "Like last night, eh? We took the risks and got us a beating and you come off without a hair out of place, eh? You figure to take over this outfit, mister?"

Blake shrugged. "Whoever does will have to keep a cool head. Going berserk is going to get everybody into a mess which we might not be able to get out of."

"You figure to bow down to these scum, Durant?" Damiani shouted at him and the rest of the men turned their heads and listened uneasily.

Blake Durant shook his head. "That never entered my head, Damiani. But what did, is that to get out of here finally a man will have to be fit enough to fight and maybe fit enough to walk fifty miles across a desert or scale a mountain to hell knows where. If the chance comes, I aim to be ready for it. So you do what you like, and I'll do what I like, Damiani, just so you leave me be."

Damiani scoffed loudly and called to the others, "Durant aims to do a full day's work for a full day's feed." His gaze picked out Curly Bromage and he went on, "What do you think about that, Curly?"

Bromage, who was being handed his plate by Josh Warlow, merely kept his eyes down and for a long moment while the others looked his way, clearly waiting for his reply, he stood there, unmoving. Then he drew himself tall and turned. He raked a quick look around the men and said, "Durant can do what he likes as far as I'm concerned, Danny. We just worry about ourselves, eh?"

He went off by himself and sat against the wall of the compound and started to eat. Danny Damiani kept studying him angrily until the rest of the men had been served and Warlow called him forward and handed him a plate of hash. Damiani sniffed it and curled his lip. Then he walked the length of the compound and threw the plate against the gate. The clatter of the plate brought a guard's head and shoulders over the wall but after a moment's silent inspection of the prisoners he vanished from sight.

Blake Durant moved forward and accepted his meal from Warlow and heard Warlow say, "Could be you'll regret that, Danny, come a day or two."

"I don't eat slops for anybody, Warlow," growled Damiani, "so shut down and leave me be. The whole damn lot of you leave me be, unless you want to do as I do. One thing's certain, I'm not making anybody work while I starve in this stinkhole."

Alone, Danny Damiani moved restlessly across the clearing of the compound, his stare always searching.

The men finished their meal and stood in line for water to drink and wash up in. When that was finished, Warlow collected the buckets and put them just inside the gateway and then retired to the wall to squat on his haunches.

Like the majority of the men, he kept looking from Damiani to Durant and back again, and a deep frown etched itself between his pain-ridden eyes.

* * *

They were coming out of the compound under armed guard in a slow-moving line when a young woman suddenly broke from the porch of the smaller of the two ranch houses.

Blake Durant had been intent on memorizing the layout of this place, working out the distance between the ranch houses, where the barn was situated, the horse yards, and more importantly, the high water tower with its two huge water storage tanks. They held enough water, he decided, to keep this establishment going for a year whether it rained or not.

It was when his study had just about finished that he returned his gaze to the smaller of the two ranch houses. Three men lazed about on the porch, two in rockers, one standing against the post at the steps.

Suddenly the door of the house opened and the young woman came running out.

She stopped momentarily when she saw the guards, then pulled a tattered shawl about her body and broke into a run. She jumped from the porch and stumbled when she hit the ground, but she was almost immediately in full stride again, heading straight for the column of prisoners.

The first of the men in the column stopped dead and the others bunched up behind him. Shouts came from the porch and a single shot was fired into the air.

The young woman, hair flying, came on and soon Blake could clearly see the marks on her face. One cheek was badly bruised and her mouth was swollen. There were also dull red marks on her neck as though she had been nearly strangled. But it was her eyes that captured and held his interest. There was a crazy gleam of desperation in them, and it seemed to him that she would come on even if hellfire was in her way.

Will Hopgood's voice sounded in a bellow. "Get her, damn you!"

Blake turned to see Hopgood running from the back of the column. Bart Gilbert was close behind him and then four other guards came running.

Curly Bromage pulled in alongside Blake and said hurriedly, "This could be our chance, Durant. If we all run now, they can't stop all of us."

Danny Damiani came up a moment later licking his lips and looking urgently about him. "Why not?" he called out. "Durant, you make for the water tower and I'll head for the barn. Curly, see if you can reach the main house. We need horses, water and guns, and then we'll blast our way outa here."

Blake was still undecided when a guard caught hold of the young woman. She flung herself at him with a clawing ferocity that for a time forced the guard to back away.

"Scum!" she screamed, breaking free of him and running on again towards the bunch of prisoners. Her hands were waving about wildly and her shawl had fallen off her shoulders showing welts along the top of her bosom above the line of her blouse. Suddenly she stopped and pointed at Torp Berry who had come onto the porch of the main ranch house.

"Animal," she cried out. "Butcher, thief, liar!"

Berry lifted a hand gun and fired a shot at her feet.

When she backed away he came off the porch. Will Hopgood had almost reached the girl but now turned his interest to the bunched men.

"Get back," he called out. "The first one who moves gets his feet shot from under him."

The men started to shuffle back into line again and Damiani snapped angrily, "Damn you, Durant, you're yeller. If you'd bought in then, we'd have made it for sure. At least one of us would have, anyway. So help me, I'll get even for this."

"We wouldn't have made it, Damiani," Blake told him calmly. "Take a look at the house the girl came from."

Damiani resentfully turned his gaze that way. The three guards who had been on the porch had returned to it, and were down on their knees, their rifles held to their shoulders. There was a calm determination in their faces that suggested they had been carefully trained to react to rebellion in just this way.

Damiani grumbled something under his breath and moved away, but Curly Bromage muttered, "You're right, Durant. Hell, don't you miss anything?"

"In the trouble we're in, Bromage," replied Blake, "it doesn't pay to overlook anything. Our time will come but we've got to wait for it and not push the issue. This is a bunch of hellions, ruled by one man. When he makes a mistake—and he will—we'll act then. Meantime we could have gotten that young woman shot down."

Curly Bromage checked on Danny Damiani who had stopped momentarily and was looking straight at the woman. Bromage informed Blake, "It's Len Soncum's girl. He was the old-timer who came hell-ridin' into town yesterday, and didn't make it."

Blake shifted so he could see the young woman better. Despite her mauled and bedraggled appearance, she still stood defiantly in front of Will Hopgood. Hopgood's eyes swept the clearing. When he was assured that the guards had control of the situation, he called out to Gilbert, "Bart, put her in the compound. Let's see if a day in the sun suits her better'n a day indoors with all the comforts she could want."

Bart Gilbert crossed to May Soncum and placed a hand on her arm. But she swung on him and clawed her nails down his face. Gilbert let out a howl of pain and swung a fist into her jaw. The young woman went down without a murmur and lay unmoving.

Blake shifted forward a pace but Curly Bromage laid a restraining hand on his forearm and when Blake looked at him for the reason, Bromage shook his head, then nodded in Damiani's direction.

"She was the reason Danny wanted to come here in the first place, Durant," he said. "She and her old man came out a week ago. Danny figured to make a play for her."

Blake watched Damiani move out of the line and stand tense as a crouching mountain lion as Gilbert pulled May to her feet. The lean gun hand then shoved his rifle into her back and forced her down the line of men. He carefully checked out Danny Damiani as he went past him. Blake saw the girl look quickly Damiani's way and her brow creased in a frown.

Then she was pushed forward roughly again. She stumbled and fell to her knees. Gilbert jerked her up again and pushed her on and she finally went from sight.

Hopgood got the column of prisoners moving again while Torp Berry returned to his ranch house. Under the continual prodding of rifles, the prisoners were forced to march into the heat of the morning. For five miles they trudged across open country until Hopgood finally called a halt at the bottom of a steep hill.

Looking up the slope, Blake saw where huge boulders had been blown from their positions. Rubble and stumps of trees, torn brush and smaller rocks littered the scarred face of the hill.

Will Hopgood was suddenly alongside Durant. He pointed upwards, and with a leering look, said, "Durant, on account of you are a real confident gent, I'm going to put you in charge of a bunch way up on top. What you do, using bars, is prise those big boulders out and send them rolling down. Take four of these fools with you and try to stop falling or getting in the way of anything that might crush you, eh? By sundown I want that whole section cleared so we can blast again tonight before we head back to the ranch."

The only sound was the rasp of the men's breathing after the punishing march. Durant's glance followed the swing of Hopgood's hand. He said nothing but his mind worked hard.

Within an hour that whole slope would be ablaze with sunlight, and the heat, as the day went on, would become increasingly unbearable until finally no man would be able to stand up there, let alone work at dislodging huge boulders.

He said, "You're loco, Hopgood."

Hopgood's eyes narrowed and his face flushed with rage. He swung his rifle and hit Blake in the ribs with the stock. Blake edged back with the blow but showed no sign of anger or pain. His stare remained fixed on Hopgood.

"Few of these men will make it past noon, Hopgood," he said flatly. "You might as well kill them now as go on with this."

The men stood back, listening, Curly Bromage at their head, his look becoming more puzzled as he heard out this argument. Hopgood swung the rifle again against Durant's ribs and again Blake Durant did not budge.

"By sundown," Durant went on solidly, "you won't have a man in this outfit who will be able to stand on his feet, Hopgood. Whatever you're looking for up there, will need a hundred fit men to unearth."

"We'll unearth it, Durant, no mistake!" bellowed Hopgood. "If it takes a week, two weeks, we'll clear that whole hill."

"Must be gold then," Blake said quietly. "Though whoever told you this was gold-bearing ore, was mistaken. Silver maybe, in small supply, perhaps some coal."

"To hell with the ore, Durant. Nobody's going mining. What we're looking for is Percy Dog..." Hopgood chopped off whatever he was about to say and sucked air into his lungs until he looked ready to explode. He then grabbed Durant by the neck and hurled him forward. As Durant stumbled, he pulled the whip from under his belt and laid the lash squarely across Durant's back. None of the other men moved.

Durant rose, his shirt torn where the lash had laid open the range-tanned flesh. He turned slowly as Hopgood slashed at him again. Durant lifted a hand and let the lash coil about his wrist and forearm. His stare was fixed solidly on Hopgood and no sign of pain, hardly any of annoyance, showed in his dark eyes. Then he yanked on the whip and brought Hopgood stumbling forward.

Hopgood let out a cry, then the whip handle was dragged from his grasp. Durant, standing tall with feet planted wide, coolly broke the stock of the whip and pulled the leather strip free. He tossed it aside and dropped the broken stock at his feet.

Gilbert and three of the guards pressed forward. Danny Damiani shifted out of the prisoner line. But Curly Bromage was quick to lay a hand on his chest and say tightly, "No, Danny."

Damiani glared furiously at him. But the click of rifle hammers took his attention back to Bart Gilbert. Gilbert had his gun pointed straight at Damiani. Another guard had his rifle levelled on Curly Bromage. A third had Durant covered.

Hopgood straightened, brushing grit off his hands and glaring at Durant. His chest heaved under the strain of his rapid breathing and his eyes were a menacing black glitter of venomous hate. "By hell, Durant," he mouthed, "I'm goin' to tear you apart!"

Hopgood came pounding forward, swinging the rifle at shoulder height. He swung the stock and Durant went under it. The momentum of Hopgood's attempt to smash in Durant's head took him off balance. Gilbert and the guards moved a step closer. Then a shot rang through the morning's silence and Hopgood regained his balance to glare about him.

Torp Berry was sitting a gray mare only fifty feet away, in the shade of a clump of old cottonwoods, his gun across the pommel of the saddle with smoke trailing from the muzzle. Berry waited for Hopgood to get a firmer grip on the rifle, before he said, "Will, you're letting your temper get the better of you. No sense in fighting any of these fools fairly. Just get them working and get our rewards from that."

Hopgood's mouth twitched with strain as he stood there clearly fighting to make a decision.

Then a wicked smile curled about his thin-lipped mouth. "Okay, Torp," he said. "Your way for two days. But if we ain't gettin' any place by then I'm goin' to take Durant apart. One more or less won't matter a spit by then."

"Exactly," said Torp Berry. He brought his horse down the grade and motioned Bart Gilbert to get the men up the slope of the hill. The guards pulled some brush away from a cache of tools at the foot of the slope and began handing out iron bars and shovels. They then took their positions in shade and settled down to keep their guns trained on the work gang.

Blake Durant climbed to the very top of the slope and looked westward. As far as he could see there was desert, endless mile upon mile of it. It was the same to the north and the south and he knew the east where they had been brought from was no better. He put down his iron bar and worked his shoulders to get the muscles moving. Then, looking down to where a sullen-faced Will Hopgood stood, he spat on his hands, picked up the bar and dug it under a huge boulder.

CHAPTER FOUR
Always the Loner

"You got to hand it to him, Curly, he's tough," said Josh Warlow.

Warlow mopped at his brow with a soiled and sweat-dampened bandanna and watched Blake Durant prise another huge boulder free. The rest of the hands were sitting in shade and had been resting for fifteen minutes.

Curly Bromage grunted agreement with Warlow's statement and painfully pushed himself to his feet. When he moved his shoulders he could feel his blood-caked whip gashes and the bullet furrow from the onslaught on the stockade gate opening again. He did not seem to mind. He went out of the shade and picked up an iron bar. Then he climbed the slope and joined Blake Durant. For one long moment, the two big men studied each other.

Then Will Hopgood came pounding halfway up the slope and called out, "Okay, Bromage, you want that, you got it. From now on when all the others rest, you and Durant can keep going. You keep going the whole damned day and we'll see how damned good you are."

Curly Bromage let a tired smile twist the corners of his mouth. His curly red hair was wet with sweat which ran down his face in rivulets.

He dug the bar under the boulder Durant was working at, and together they heaved back until their muscles creaked, but the boulder wouldn't shift.

They exchanged another look and Bromage said, "Knew a jasper once who could turn over a wagon single-handed, Durant. Big man, near as big as you and me."

Blake gave him a grin, and put the iron bar under the rock on his side and worked it deeper into the clay. Sweat dripped from his brow and chin. Bromage gritted his teeth and worked for a whole minute getting a better hold for the bar, before he gave Durant a terse nod.

Both big men heaved back a second time. A sound almost like a groan came from under the rock as if some long-imprisoned ghost had finally been set free. The boulder shifted, hung on a point a moment, then went forward. Bromage and Durant, working together, kept the pressure on and the boulder rolled right over, stopped for a moment poised on a point of balance, and then began to slowly gather pace.

Watching from below, Will Hopgood realized with a start that the boulder was coming faster than he had expected. He scrambled to the side of the slope as the boulder, bringing a storm of rubble and brush and stumps with it, rushed down towards him. Hopgood flung himself urgently sideways as the boulder pounded past. He hit the ground on his stomach and his rifle exploded in his hand.

When he got to his feet and the dust had settled, he glared upwards to where Durant and Bromage were already working to free another boulder.

Hopgood licked his lips and wiped his face with his sleeve and swore violently. Then, finding his own men looking curiously at him, he bellowed, "Okay, get them all working. Keep them at it. We got us a pair of real strong men up there, so we let them set the pace. They stop to swallow, either of them, by hell, give it to them!"

Josh Warlow, Danny Damiani and the others slowly drew themselves to their feet. The men already looked beat. But they dragged themselves into position and picked up their tools. The noon sun beat down mercilessly but on top of the hill Curly Bromage and Blake Durant did not seem affected by it. They did not speak to each other because both felt there was no energy to waste up there. They sweated and suffered and worked and continually checked on each other to make best use of their combined efforts.

* * *

Torp Berry watched the tall, lean cowhand come across the clearing from the compound where he had been sent to check on May Soncum. The cowhand's face, which Berry remembered had never looked happy at any time, was now plainly sullen. The man looked at the ground as he came as if seeking some advice from the hard-baked clay. And when he stopped before the porch steps, his gaze lifted so slowly, Berry could feel the stare digging at his ankles, legs, thighs, middle and chest before it settled, deeply worried, on his face.

"Well?" he asked.

"There ain't no shade in there, Mr. Berry," the cowhand said. "She'll likely get sun-loco."

"Likely," Berry said, unconcerned.

The cowhand shook his head and looked troubled. "I don't figure that's right. I don't figure a lot of things are right here, like last night letting Hopgood maul her. She ain't no more than a spit of a girl."

"And pretty enough for you to want, Conachie?" Berry taunted the lean man.

Conachie's eyebrows met in the middle of his forehead. His balding head became a mass of wrinkles. "Ain't that at all, and you know it, Mr. Berry. But where I come from, men respect their womenfolk. We come out here for gold and same as the rest I want my share. If we got to kill a couple of troublesome jaspers, I guess that's only part and passel of the deal. But I don't like it when a woman's mauled, and sent crazy and left to suffer like Miss Soncum is. She ain't done nothin' to deserve that kind of treatment."

Torp Berry smiled crookedly. "Nor her pa?" he asked.

Conachie's head lifted with a jerk and his eyes filled with deeper worry. "Her pa is a different thing, Mr. Berry," he argued.

Berry pushed himself to his feet, shaking his head. His smile remained fixed on Conachie's haggard, drawn features. "Her pa was a different thing, Conachie," he said a moment later as he leaned across the porch rail. "Len Soncum is dead. Soncum made the mistake of breaking out of here before he was told he could leave. He also made the mistake of bucking me in town and trying to kill me. Well, for your information, Conachie, since you didn't travel to town with us, he didn't make it. We shot him down like the troublesome old jasper he always proved to be. *You* reckon that's good riddance to a pest like him?"

Conachie licked his lips and rubbed a tired hand across his fleshless face. High cheekbones and protruding jaw were rims to the hollows of his old face.

"Guess he got what he deserved," Conachie said uneasily.

Berry lifted his gun and trained it on his hired hand. His gaze went suddenly hard. "Everybody gets what he deserves, Conachie, especially those who are left to stand guard on an old man and his daughter and let the old man escape."

Conachie took a quick step backwards and shook his head in fright. His eyes widened to push his wrinkled forehead right into his bald head. "No, Mr. Berry," he said. "You got it wrong. Miss Soncum, she wanted to have a bath and I fetched her some water and two others was still with her when we found old Soncum missing. His horse was gone, too."

Conachie continued, "I had a hell of a time keeping Shepherd and O'Shea off Miss Soncum like you said I was to do."

Berry fired a shot. The bullet hit Conachie in the middle and sent him staggering. But he did not go down. He stood there, clutching his stomach, the blood pouring over his bony fingers. All color went from his face until he looked like a bag of bones with a skeletal head perched on it.

Berry fired again, this time putting the shot through Conachie's neck. Conachie went down, making a gurgling sound. He dug his hands into the earth as two other men came from the shade at the side of the old ranch house. Berry looked disinterestedly at them, before he gave Conachie one last, disdainful look.

Then he said, "Bury him where you like, and while you're at it, thank your lucky stars it isn't you going under the sod."

Jake Shepherd and Larry O'Shea came forward hesitantly and picked up Conachie's bleeding body from the hard-baked ground. When they looked nervously at the porch again, Torp Berry was gone from sight. They heard the pop of a cork and then the pouring of a drink. Without a word they carried their burden behind the old ranchhouse and dug a grave.

* * *

May Soncum lowered her hands from the top of her head as the compound gates opened. She saw Jake Shepherd first, the runt of a man who the previous day had followed her about all the time, ogling her, his thoughts mirrored in his mean, wasted features. Then Larry O'Shea came up behind him, a big man, with long dangling arms and a crazed, lustful look in his hooded eyes. It was O'Shea who had once made a grab at her and torn her blouse from her body and then stood there, unmoving, as if he was seeing a naked woman for the first time. She could still feel the sting in her hand as she hit him with all her might and sent him backing off.

A deep fear rushed into May Soncum. So it was to be another mauling, she told herself, and after what Hopgood had done to her the previous evening and the hardship she had been through this day, she knew she had no strength to fight them off.

"Animals!" she screamed out at the top of her voice and her cry had barely begun to die in the heat-soaked air when Torp Berry came into the gateway.

Berry made a signal and O'Shea and Shepherd went away, closing the gate behind them. Berry carried a canteen in one hand. He stopped a few yards short of May and uncorked the canteen and drank greedily, letting water spill down his chin and soak into his shirt.

May felt her mouth contract and her lips crack. She had not had anything to drink all day and already it was past noon. Or she thought it was.

She realized with a shock that she was hardly certain of anything anymore, not even if she was May Soncum, daughter of Len Soncum, come all this way out here to make their fortune.

"Drink, May?"

Berry was holding the canteen towards her. May looked at it and then at him. His hand was steady and there was no hint of mockery in his face.

She reached for the canteen and he pulled it back, slowly, his eyes gleaming with satisfaction as a cry of dismay came from her.

"Leave me be then," May begged him. She pulled away from him and finally turned and hid her face against the stockade wall. Deep sobs came from between her clenched teeth.

"May, you've been downright foolish," Berry said chidingly. "I treated you right. I gave you every comfort I could and the promise of more when this stint was over. All you did was spit in my face."

"I'm a human being," she said. "I have my rights. I can't, just can't let any man..." Her voice trailed off and she looked imploringly at him.

Berry shrugged. "I guess in a way that's right, May. You have a choice. It's move back into the house with me or stay here with these other prisoners."

"If you do the former, I swear no harm will come to you. I'll do anything you wish when you are my woman, and nobody else's."

"You... can say that?" May cried. "After last night? After you let that swine, that cowardly, blustering, filthy-mannered Hopgood attack me?"

"That was a regrettable incident, May," Berry told her easily. "But there will be no more of that. Will knows where he stands. He was going loco anyway, not being able to get to you. Well, I guess he's satisfied himself and that's the end of it. I'll tell him so anyway, so come on now, come to the house, clean up, get some rest, water and food and everything will be fine again."

May shook her head quickly. "I couldn't ... I just couldn't. Where is pa? What have you done to him?"

Berry's face clouded. "It's that, I said, or stay here with these desperate jaspers, all of whom will probably know their time is up here and they might as well take what they can get while they can get it. You know very little about menfolk, May. Every damned man on this ranch wants you so bad, he'll kill to get you. So you need my protection. As my woman, nobody would dare molest you."

May moved slightly back towards him and extended her hand. "May I have a drink then?"

Berry's eyes lit up. "You mean it?"

May nodded and licked her dry lips. Berry handed her the canteen. She lifted the neck to her lips and drank slowly, taking her fill. When she lowered the canteen, her eyes went suddenly and blazingly wide.

"Why, you filthy swine, Berry, and fool into the bargain," she said. "Do you think for one moment that I could let you touch me? My skin would crawl. I'd shrivel up and die inside before I'd give in to you."

May hurled the canteen at him. Berry ducked and then swung a backhand at her. May was knocked off her feet.

"Coward!" she screamed. "Old men and women are your victories. You need gun hands for the rest. You are the most despicable scum I have ever met in my life and that includes your friend, Hopgood. You make a good pair, the jackal and the hyena."

Berry stepped forward and hit her again and when she fell sideways he kicked her in the ribs. Then, as May groaned, on the point of unconsciousness, he tore her blouse off her and hurled it across the yard. He stood there, feeling the sun burning the back of his neck before he heeled about and left the stockade.

* * *

Blake Durant felt as if fires were burning under his skin. His hands were swollen and torn and he could scarcely hold the iron bar any longer.

Every time he leaned forward to dig the bar into the rocky ground he felt as if he would topple forward on his face.

Curly Bromage had already done that twice in the last ten minutes, proving to Durant that Bromage, after a day of working to the utmost in defiance of Will Hopgood and his armed guards, had finally reached the end of his tether.

Now Bromage lay motionless to his right while Will Hopgood came hurrying up the slope, wheezing with the effort of climbing. He gave Blake Durant a careful look before he toed Bromage in the ribs. Curly Bromage did not stir. The late sunlight streamed over his bloodied back making the bruises and gashes more distinct and more ugly.

Hopgood toed him again, a little harder this time. Durant put down his bar and leaned on it. His face was completely expressionless when he said, "He's had enough."

"To hell he has," growled Hopgood. "You ain't cleared but two-thirds of this damned top. I said I wanted the lot cleared."

"I'm beaten, too, Hopgood," Blake told him easily. "If I'm pushed any more today I might not come up tomorrow. Then where would you be? What would Berry say to that?"

"To hell with Berry," said Hopgood. "I'm running this show. The gold's under that shoulder and I aim to get it."

"Before the rains?" Blake asked him. He looked at the rim of the slope where a gathering of black clouds darkened the sundown. But Blake knew that this was only a forerunner to a storm, a gathering that would deepen and increase every day until finally the clouds would burst. How long, he could not be sure, but he suspected that before the week was out this place would be a quagmire.

Hopgood scowled blackly at him and then studied the rain clouds, too. Unlike Blake Durant he had not spent much time weighing up the signs of the country. It either rained or it didn't, that was all he knew.

"And since it's right important to get this work done before the storm, Hopgood," Blake told him, "I advise you to lay off the men. We'll work, sure, because there seems no other way out of it. But, by hell, you can push a man only so far when he doesn't care any more about living or dying." Blake showed him his hands. "These will need salt to dry them out and salve to soften them or I won't be able to pick up a bar tomorrow. If I can't, nobody else will and you'll have Berry to answer to."

"I said, damn you, Durant," Hopgood shouted, "to hell with Berry! He don't run this outfit the way he figures he does. I'm the boss man out here and what I say goes!"

"Suit yourself," Blake said and reached back to pick up his range coat. He looked thoughtfully at the prostrate and unmoving Curly Bromage and, with a faint smile twisting his mouth, said, "Push him too far, mister, and he'll come at you with his bare hands. You saw him today, saw the pride he has in himself. I think that pride goes deep enough for him to keep walking through any kind of hell to get to somebody he wanted to kill."

Hopgood licked his lips and stepped back a pace. Then he looked anxiously about him. Gilbert and the other guards had collected the men down near the timber. Gilbert was laying out explosives and fitting fuses. When he paused to look up towards Durant and Hopgood, Hopgood said, "Okay, Durant, I'll play along with that for now. Get that weakling out of here and then mind your manners. I'm not going to be taken in by you and your damned easy manner. You was hurt today, mister, hurt bad. And tomorrow it'll be worse, the next day worse again. By hell, I'm going to cut you down to size or die trying, Durant."

"Try all you like, Hopgood, but you won't succeed," Blake said calmly. He pulled the unconscious Bromage up off the ground and worked him across his shoulder. He brushed Hopgood aside and struggled down the slope towards the other men. Josh Warlow came forward to help him lower Bromage to the ground, and when Warlow saw the pain etched into Curly Bromage's features, he snapped a curse and yelled:

"Damn you to hell, Hopgood! You're a fiend!"

Will Hopgood scowled blackly down for a minute before amusement sparked in his eyes. "There'll be worse, Warlow, for all of you," he said. "Not enough done today. Reckon tomorrow, when it gets real hot, all of you can come up here and finish this place off." He wiped sweat from his face and told Bart Gilbert to come up. Gilbert spent half an hour laying out his explosives before he lit the fuses and with Hopgood pounding in front of him, came down the slope at a sliding run. They forced the prisoners into a dry creek bed, and had the guards positioned to cover them.

No sooner had Hopgood's head gone down into the cover of a tree stump than a terrific explosion shook the ground. Rubble came scattering down near them, followed by larger chunks of rock. The echo of the explosion hung in the air for a long time before it slowly died.

Hopgood was the first to his feet and hurried back to the hill. After a brief inspection he told Gilbert, "You done it good, Bart. Got enough of a hole up there to be near the bottom. Another day, and I reckon we'll hit the floor of the cave. Got to."

Bart Gilbert looked uncertainly up at the scarred mountain. To his mind, more than half the hill had been blown away, yet there seemed no limit to the depth he would have to go. He wiped a hand tiredly across his weathered face and brought his gun to bear on Blake Durant.

Curly Bromage, after a drink from a guard's canteen, had recovered. He stood there, glaring at Hopgood, bloodied hands clenched as though he was clutching Hopgood's throat.

Blake Durant nudged him and began to walk, and, without a word from the guards, the prisoners formed a line and followed the big man, Blake Durant, in a shambling walk back to camp.

* * *

They were put into the stockade and promised a meal and water as soon as the guards had fed themselves. Blake headed for the far wall, wanting to be alone to do some solid thinking when he sighted a form huddled against the stockade wall. But before he could make out who it was, Danny Damiani brushed past him.

Grinning widely, Damiani said, "Damn me, it's the Soncum girl!"

CHAPTER FIVE
Outlaw Gold

Danny Damiani dropped down beside the
unconscious May Soncum and studied her admiringly.
There was sufficient light still left in the evening for
him to make out the smoothly rounded contours of her
naked breasts. His eyes gleamed with interest as his
hand stole onto the right breast and he fondled it while
pretending to draw her into a sitting position.

Blake Durant's hand fell on his shoulder and with
a jerk Durant brought him back onto his haunches.
He took off his hide coat and dropped it over the girl's
upper body.

Damiani swung about, face flushed with anger.
When he saw who had pulled him, he snarled, "By hell,
Durant, you've asked for it now."

"Leave her be," Blake told him. "She's been through
enough. We all heard what happened last night. It won't
happen here."

Damiani came to his feet, fists bunched. "You the top
man all of a sudden, Durant?" he growled.

"I won't see a defenseless woman hurt more than
she has already been, Damiani. Keep your hands off
her."

"You're tellin' me, drifter?"

"I'm telling you, Damiani."

The other men stood back in a circle watching each of these two men in turn. Silence settled heavily on the whole group and Danny Damiani worked a little way off from Durant and smirked.

"So you're tellin' me, eh, Durant?" he mocked. "When we raided the gate last night you kept out of it. When me and Curly and Josh was whipped you didn't do a damned thing to help us, did you? Then today you did everything Hopgood asked of you, worked real fine, like you was one of them, maybe."

"Last night was fool's work, Damiani, and was proved to be so. The whipping business was your own fault for bucking these jaspers futilely. If anybody had gone to your assistance they would have been shot. I don't think there's a man who didn't want to do something. As for today, the one way out of here is to get these scum off their guard. By pretending to—"

"Pretending?" Damiani threw scornfully at him, and turned to grin at Curly Bromage. "Now, ain't you something, mister. Well, you might have a couple of these men fooled but you ain't foolin' me one spit. You're yeller, Durant, clear through."

"No," Curly Bromage said quietly and brought Damiani's stare raking over him. "Durant's anything but that, Danny, and you best remember it."

"You better also remember this ain't no open country where a gun rules the roost. In a town maybe or on a ranch where men can do what they like, you hold all the ace cards. But here, locked up where there ain't no guns, we got to think different. I think Durant's thinking right and until he proves he ain't, then I'm going along with what he does."

Danny Damiani glared at his trail friend. "You turnin' on me, Curly? You forgettin' how we stood before we came here, my gun making things easy for us." Damiani spat on the ground. "By hell, maybe the rest of you are fooled by Durant, too. Ain't you got no sense? He's a saddlebum, came riding into Maple with a fool message from my pa. Then he messed up his chance when Berry got the drop on us, and didn't prove himself no ways a man to me. I'm sayin' it loud and clear," he went on, "while we're here, there ain't nothin' changed from what it was before. I give the orders, all the way and the man who bucks that can answer to me for it later. As for the Soncum girl, she's mine. I set my hat for her back in Maple when she came through. You all knew that, knew that was why I came on this fool signup in the first place." Damiani's eyes darkened and his lips peeled back derisively when he looked at Durant. "So all of you get and keep to hell outa my hair."

Curly Bromage frowned and looked straight at Blake Durant. Blake stood with his hands at his sides and returned his look calmly.

"Touch her and I'll kill you, Damiani," he said tightly. "As for the rest, do what you like and I'll do what I like. But don't expect me to throw in with any fool schemes which might get me killed for no chance of success."

Blake turned away and three of the older men went with him. When Blake sat down with his back to the stockade wall, watching Damiani carefully, Curly Bromage crossed to him and sat opposite him. Soon, every other man there came and joined them.

It was Josh Warlow who asked, "You got anything in mind, Durant?"

Blake shook his head. "Nope."

Warlow looked troubled. "Then why throw in with them without a fight, Durant?"

Blake shrugged and looked at the high walls. "There's no way out except through the gate. Even if we managed to get through it, we'd have to run through a barrage of rifle shots. If we cleared that there's desert on all sides, and we'd need water and horses or there wouldn't be any one of us reach Maple alive."

Warlow sucked his gums and tugged at his gray hair. He looked ten years older than when Durant had seen him in the Maple saloon.

"That don't answer him fully, Durant," Curly Bromage put in. "I'm not going all the way with Danny, but hell, I ain't going through what I went through today again, either. I guess I just worked with you to prove something to myself which got well and truly proved. You're tough, Durant, and I don't reckon you got any coward streak in you. But by hell you got me confused. You aim to fight finally?"

"Sure."

"When?"

"I don't know, Bromage. All I'm waiting for is for one of them to get careless. I thought about using the bars out there today, but that wouldn't work, and some of the other men would have gotten killed. It's no use running into the brush, either. Berry and his scum would hunt us down and kill us or worse." Blake sat back and sighed wearily. "We'll just have to wait, or I will, anyway. I'm not asking anybody else to do what I'm doing or to listen to me. Each man thinks for himself as far as I'm concerned."

An old man came shambling up to study Blake Durant very seriously. "I been watchin' you all since you came, especially you, Durant. I been thinking about a lot of things, like the crowd I came with a week ago. Only me and old Moose left now of that lot... eleven of us. Name's Tom Seeney. My boy, Jesse, he was a wild one, couldn't take anybody tellin' him what to do, ever, not even his ma or me."

Seeney continued, "Jesse lost his temper and rushed Hopgood and was shot clear through the middle. Took four men with him in that fight. All of them was killed. Then we was all lined up and flogged. Ben Adamson, he died from that. Left five of us. Moose and me and three others. We was made to work in the heat, twelve hours a day. The others couldn't take it and run off. Hopgood shot them down like dogs. Then we was bundled back into here and left without water for three days. No grub either. Moose and me, we ain't got no fight left in us."

All the men eyed the old man. His clothes were tatters on his frame and his face looked like it belonged to a corpse. His hands constantly trembled and his lips quivered. "Moose and me, we just been talking, Durant," the old man continued, "and for what it's worth we reckon you're handling this the right way. Hopgood ain't a man to trust anybody but I reckon you beat him today. He knows that what you did he couldn't do and none of his men could do. You won a point, mister, which just might help get us all out of here. Those guards are dead scared of you already and when a man gets scared he makes mistakes. Durant, you're right, and if these men ever want to see a town again, they best follow you all the way."

Tom Seeney turned and studied Danny Damiani solidly before his lips curled back scornfully. "You, Damiani, you're a fool clear through. You keep your mouth shut and, like Durant says, you leave that little girl alone."

"She's got enough to worry about, all of us men here knowing about last night. You hurt her, embarrass her in any way and you got a lot of these men, maybe all of them, to contend with."

Danny Damiani leaped to his feet and charged across the clearing. But before he could close on Tom Seeney, Curly Bromage stepped between them. Bromage did no more than shake his head, but his face had gone white and his lips were no more than a thin line in his tight-featured face.

"Get outa my way, Curly," Damiani said. "Git now!"

"No, Danny. Leave him be. I reckon he spoke for all of us."

"You reckon—" began Danny Damiani and he reached out and grabbed Bromage by the shoulder. Bromage stood there, holding his stare locked in his own. He made no attempt to prise the grip off his shoulder nor did he seem in any way affected by the threat of assault.

"This is a no-gun territory, Danny," he said quietly. "Play it that way."

"Okay," he muttered. "Okay. I know every damn one of you. Those who come on my side can ride with me when we get out. Those who don't, by hell..." Damiani's mouth twisted sourly and he looked straight at Bromage. "Those who don't, Curly, can ride to the devil," he concluded.

Damiani turned and walked slowly back to May Soncum. She had begun to stir. She watched him frowningly, plainly unable to understand where she was or who he was. Damiani dropped down beside her and said quietly, "I'm Danny Damiani. I met you in Maple a week ago, come out here to help you."

"Help?" she asked and looked anxiously about her. The tall walls seemed to remind her of tragic things. "How?"

"Just leave it to me, Miss Soncum. There's scum here who want you, but ain't nobody goin' to hurt you, 'cept over my dead body."

May looked heavily at him, still apparently stunned by the misfortunes of the last couple of days. "My father?" she asked him. "Do you know my father? Do you know what happened to him?"

"He's dead, ma'am," Damiani said and saw the color drain from her face. By hell, she was a looker, he told himself, or would be when she cleaned up and dressed up and had some rest. Just the kind he had always looked for but until he had made a name for himself as a gun, the kind who had never taken any notice of him.

"Dead? Pa is dead?" she said faintly.

"Berry shot him down in town. Your pa died right, if that means anything to you, ma'am."

"Mean anything?" May asked and fell back against the wall with a pained cry coming from her lips. "What can anything mean without pa? Oh, my God!"

"Things are on the improve, ma'am," Damiani tried to console her. "You just trust in me. Don't have no truck with anybody else. It's you and me, and by hell I'll get Berry for you and Hopgood and the rest of this miserable bunch. I'll get you away, sure."

May did not look up. She folded her hands on her lap and for the first time realized she had a coat about her shoulders. With a shock she realized that underneath it she was naked. She remembered then the terrible incident with Torp Berry. Never before in her life had she wanted to kill anybody but right then she knew, given a chance, she would kill Berry any way she could.

"Is this your coat?" she asked Damiani, and Damiani, after checking to see if anybody was close, nodded. "You've got nothing to worry about any more," he told her. "They're going to bring us some grub and water soon. You just rest and when it comes, stay here. I'll see you right, ma'am."

May closed her eyes. Her whole body sagged and for a moment Danny Damiani thought she had passed out again. He sat still, muscles taut, and thought about what he would do to Curly Bromage. And to Blake Durant. And to the whole lot of this bunch who had deserted him.

The day of the gun would come again, just as soon as the day of the damned was finished. He rested back, drawing the cool evening air into his lungs.

* * *

Torp Berry paced the floor of his living room, continually frowning. Will Hopgood, glass in hand, sat on the divan and Bart Gilbert, also with a glass, rested against the doorway jamb, listening to the restless pounding of Berry's steps on the carpeted floor.

Gilbert was thinking of the gold under the pile of huge boulders which had a year or so ago come tumbling down from the higher ridgeline to completely entomb the outlaw gold of Percy Dog Jones. How Berry had gotten wind of the hidden gold, Gilbert had no idea. But he had seen the map, with the desert sketched in accurately. There had been the big hill, with the towering flat ridge over it. Only when they had come out here, the ridge had already collapsed and buried the gold. Only explosives and a great deal of manpower could ever unearth it.

So Berry had formed a kind of syndicate, with Will Hopgood, as ramrod, and seven hired guns to act as guards. From there on it had been a simple thing to lure men out here, throw them in a compound, keep them hungry and thirsty and work them to death. Nine men had died in the process, but Gilbert saw nothing wrong with this.

More had died in the useless war between the States and more were dying every day along the frontier, in arguments that usually meant nothing more than who owned a steer or a horse and who didn't.

So Bart Gilbert had long since decided that life was a very expendable thing, if it wasn't his own. A chill went down his spine and his mind went back to the activity of the day. By hell, that Durant had proved himself all right, he thought. Bart Gilbert swore that whenever Durant was within a spit of him, he would have his gun trained on him. He didn't even give a damn what Torp Berry said. If Durant showed any signs at all of coming at him, Bart Gilbert was going to kill him and take the consequences later.

He finished his drink and turned back to look at Hopgood and Berry. The argument between these two was finished, but Gilbert sensed that it still raged inside each man's mind. Berry wanted the men fed better so that more work could be got out of them. And Hopgood wanted them starved down to a point where they could hardly stand and hence be easier to control. But Gilbert, although he would never admit it to Hopgood, sided with Berry. Berry was smart. An ex-lawman, he knew the limits a prisoner could be pushed to. Also he was ruthlessly cunning, a wily one, a man who did a heap of thinking before he made up his mind on any decision.

"So we feed 'em and they get fat, and maybe they'll get so damned healthy they'll figure to rush us," Hopgood suddenly exclaimed. "You still figure you can trust the others?"

"Why shouldn't I trust them, Will?" Torp Berry asked him. "What has any of them done wrong?"

"They haven't had the chance, Torp," Hopgood went on. "Thanks to me and nobody else."

"I'll go along with that, Will," Torp Berry said easily, and crossed to refill his glass. "You've done everything I expected of you, in town and out here. But listen to me, Will. We need manpower, and we've got the only guns out here. Give them all the food they want, keep the flesh on their bodies and the strength inside them. You can work it off as you like for the next couple of days. But no water. From now on, water is out. Next time I visit the diggings I want to see them begging for a drink."

Hopgood looked placated although he threw down his drink and dropped his glass carelessly onto the table again. He then worked his big hands through his thinning hair and nodded at Gilbert.

"Give them their grub, Bart," he said, "then chain them up. Leave the girl loose so she can move about and worry the hell outa them."

Torp Berry watched his ramrod move out onto the porch. He had the sudden unsettling feeling that Hopgood held more sway with the men than he did. When they got their hands on the gold that might prove a little troublesome unless he watched himself.

So somehow, between this night and the finding of the hidden outlaw gold, he would have to pull Hopgood down a peg and regain his authority completely.

To this end, he opened the cabinet and took out four bottles of whisky. Carrying these, he left the ranch house and crossed the clearing to the guards' quarters. Finding the place empty he put the bottles down on the table and closed the door after him. He then went up to the stockade where four guards stood with rifles trained on a line of prisoners. He told them about the whisky and then went inside to inspect May Soncum again.

May, still wearing Blake Durant's hide coat, looked a lot more composed than she had been since coming out here. From the very beginning she had been trouble, he decided now. And he blamed himself for that, for not getting rid of Len Soncum and without her knowing. But even so, with womanizers like Hopgood and Gilbert in his outfit, he realized he should have deprived himself of her company and got rid of her, too. Later, when he had the gold, he could go to any place and get whatever women he liked.

"Changed your mind, May?" he asked her.

May Soncum looked defiantly back at him. "You know I never will, Berry. Can't you leave it at that?"

"Sure, sure," Berry said easily and studied the line of gaunt, hungry men with amusement. "Hope for your sake they can, May. But anyway, to prove I'm not the fiend I've been claimed to be, I'm going to chain them all up tonight. You can roam about free."

May looked curiously at him. "What are you up to now?" she asked.

For answer, Torp Berry merely smiled at her and went away. He watched Josh Warlow dishing out the meals and handing out the filled plates. Still amused, he left the stockade and studied the sky.

The storm clouds had, as they did every evening, gone away. But there was a lot of heat still in the day and he knew with absolute certainty that before the end of the week the rains would come. Then there would be no chance at all of working on the hill. In fact, rain could undermine all the work they had done thus far. It might even cause another landslide which might bury the gold forever.

Worried over that, he walked across the clearing towards the main ranch house in time to see Will Hopgood coming out of the guards' quarters carrying the bottles of whisky he'd left there for them. Torp Berry was on the point of shouting to Hopgood to take them back, when a commotion broke out in the stockade. He could hear Danny Damiani's voice loudly berating Gilbert because of the gun hand's refusal to bring water.

A shot was fired and then the four guards, closely followed by Gilbert, came out of the stockade. The gate was closed quickly and the heavy timber bars thrown back in place.

Gilbert, picking up the empty bucket which rattled with the tin plates inside it, came fast across the clearing, plainly wanting to be done with the stockade and its trouble for the night.

He stopped near Torp Berry and said, "They're in a mean mood tonight, Torp. By hell, something's got to be done about Damiani. If he ever gets a chance he'll come at us for sure and he'll take some stopping."

"With his bare hands?" Torp Berry asked him quietly.

Gilbert shrugged. "I guess not, but hell I don't like the way things are shaping lip. Those explosives I set off this evening didn't do more than shift the rocks from one place to another. Things are going too slow."

"Everything is going as I planned it, Bart," Berry told him. "So quit worryin'. You chain those fools up?"

"Sure."

"They ate the slops?"

"Yeah."

Berry grinned at him. "Then put on two of the guards to walk the outside wall, and go with the rest to Hopgood's room. You'll find he's got four bottles of whisky for you. Drink your fill, have yourselves a last time with the women and then get a good night's rest. Two, three days from now we'll be set up for life."

"Last time with the women, you said, Torp? How come?"

"I'm sending them on to Lusc to wait for us there, Bart. I don't want any more complications than are necessary until the week's end. Move on now."

Gilbert was going past Torp Berry when the tall, lean man stopped him suddenly. Gilbert looked up frowningly.

"How many plates did you take in there, Bart?"

Gilbert looked down into the bucket. He gave a muffled oath. "By hell," he swore. "Some of them damn—"

Berry pushed him aside and grabbed two of the other guards. "Get that gate open, fast!" he yelled.

The guards ran forward and worked the planks loose. Drawing his own hand gun, Torp Berry strode into the stockade as soon as the gate swung back. Gilbert, having dropped the bucket outside the wall, moved forward to join him. The prisoners chained to the iron rings on the stockade wall looked curiously back at them.

Berry gestured impatiently towards Bart Gilbert. "Search them, damn you, Bart. And bring every smart jasper to me."

Gilbert hurried to obey. He found a plate in Josh Warlow's possession and another in Danny Damiani's. Unchaining them he dragged them to their feet. Berry hurled the plates behind him where one of the guards picked them up.

"That all, Bart?" he asked.

Gilbert nodded. Torp Berry eyed Damiani viciously before he slammed his gun-loaded fist into the dark-skinned gun hand's jaw. Damiani went down and Berry moved into him and kicked brutally at his ribs and finally stamped on his face with his boot-heel.

Damiani rolled onto his side, tried vainly to rise, then slumped back unconscious.

Meanwhile, Josh Warlow, eyes wide with fright, said urgently, "I did the serving, Berry. Hell, I didn't have time to finish my meal. Gilbert grabbed up the plates before I could clean my grub up. You got no cause to—"

Berry smashed his fist into Warlow's jaw, then kept hitting him until he had him backed up against the stockade wall. He gave the old man a final heavy blow on the mouth and, still consumed with overpowering anger, kneed him in the groin.

He then turned to the others. "Be told now!" he shouted. "Next time any of you make trouble here, I'm going to kill you. The playin's over. You buck me, in any damned way at all, and blood will flow."

The prisoners looked coldly back at him. Berry swung about, gave the prostrate Damiani another kick in the stomach and told Gilbert to chain him and Warlow up again. That done he marched the guards out of the compound and waited for the gate to be closed and barred. Then, without a word, rubbing his knuckles as he went, he stormed back to the main ranch house.

CHAPTER SIX
Killing Comes Easy to Some

May Soncum moved slowly across to Danny Damiani's side. She lifted his head from the ground and with difficulty, propped him up against the stockade wall. Damiani gave out a groan and his head fell forward on his chest. Next man along the wall was Blake Durant and May's worried look went to him.

"He'll make out," Durant told her in an attempt to alleviate her concern. "He's tougher than most."

"He's bleeding badly from the nose and mouth, Mr. Durant," May said. "What should I do?"

"Just keep his head up and wait for him to come out of it. A piece of your petticoat might help stem the flow of blood."

May still wore his coat, which she had belted securely around her waist. She held his look a moment longer before she turned away and tore a piece of her undergarment away. Making a pad of it, she dabbed at Damiani's nose and his mouth. When he stirred, resting back, breathing heavily, she pushed the pad into his hand and made to go away.

But Damiani placed a hand on her wrist and shook his head. May remained kneeling there, her gaze continually shifting to take in the tall, good-looking man next to them.

Somehow she felt that he was the leader here although Damiani had professed to be that.

She reminded herself that Damiani had also told her to trust him, that he would get her away from this terrible place. She had believed him at first, mainly because she was willing to believe anybody in a desperate hope to be saved further brutalities.

But now she realized that his attempt to hide a tin plate had been the action of a man as desperate in his plight as she herself was. What he hoped to achieve she did not know, but against chains, stockade walls, and men armed with rifles she could not believe any man to be so stupid as to hope to achieve anything with a tin plate.

"Are you all right?" she asked Danny Damiani.

"Will be," Damiani growled. "You just sit there and give me a couple of minutes. I ain't licked yet, far from it, you'll see."

May was silent for a long moment before she decided that talk of any kind to any person was better than the interminable and depressing silence which had settled on the others. She noticed that the other man who had kept back a plate from the guards was already sitting up, not nearly as hurt as Damiani was.

"Why did you do it?" she asked him calmly.

"Had to," he muttered. "I've got to try anything. I could have sharpened the side of that plate and given it a cutting edge. Might even have been able to scratch through these walls with it. It doesn't matter that they got it back... something else will crop up."

"Don't you think it's all so futile, Mr. Damiani?" she asked him. "Next time they will kill you."

"If a man don't fight, Miss Soncum, he ain't worth a spit. I'll get out of here, you'll see, and so help me, a lot of scum are going to be sorry then. I've had my share of beatings before and reckon there could be some more in store for me. So what? I'll repair and when I get me someplace where I can stand on even terms with these scum, a lot of blood is going to flow. Their damned blood."

May felt a chill run through her. She sat there, as miserable as she had ever been in her life. That life, she remembered sadly, had never been so wonderful anyway, with always traipsing about the country with her father, chasing up leads to hidden treasure, gold caches, glory hole after glory hole. None of the leads had ever amounted to anything. It was only when her father had promised that this was to be his last search for a fortune that she had agreed to come with him at all. There had been very little comfort in her life and very little happiness. But her father had promised to change all that.

And now he was dead, and she was alone, with a bunch of men who could not help her at all. She had been raped, brutally beaten and humiliated. She rubbed her hands together to get the hard-caked dust off them before she fussed with her hair. Even in this terrible place she wanted to keep her pride in herself intact.

Damiani watched her closely, his aches slowly forgotten. His gaze ran down her body and he remembered how she had looked when he had first come into the stockade that night. He remembered, too, how her breast had felt under his touch. He caught her gaze and held it and a thin smile moved onto his bruised and swollen lips.

May moved back from him, suddenly alarmed by the intensity of his stare. She could almost read his thoughts and the horror she had endured with Will Hopgood came back to her in all its frightening intensity.

Blake Durant, who had been watching her carefully all this time, now called out, "Damiani, if any of us are to get out of here you and I have to come to an understanding."

May looked across at Durant, and was strangely encouraged by his coolness and confident tone.

But Damiani scowled, forced himself into a more comfortable sitting position and answered gruffly, "Durant, you and me have got nothing in common and never had. For mine, you're yeller, clear through. So why should I trade talk with you?"

"Because what I plan to do and what you are doing all the time are in conflict, Damiani. The more you buck these jaspers, the less chance my plan has of coming off."

"Plan? What damn plan, Durant? You going to lick their boots, shake their hands maybe, tell them no harm done so far?"

"Nope, Damiani," Blake said easily. "But I need your help to keep them off their guard. Another beating isn't going to do you or anybody else any good. The more you sass them, the more they're going to concentrate on guarding us. Give them a breather, let them relax, and maybe they'll relax too much. I'm afraid there's no other way for it."

Damiani scoffed at the suggestion. "You're afraid all right, Durant, right down to your boots. So hear me, mister, and hear me good. I'll do what I damned well like and you can go to blazes."

Blake Durant nodded grimly as if he had expected no reply but the one Damiani had given him.

"Then, mister," he said very quietly, "I'll have to tame you. Too many lives are involved. Your men are already disenchanted with you because you're acting like a fool. You got Warlow into trouble again, and I don't think he'll have any part of you from now on. As for the others, Bromage included, they're going to follow me."

Durant continued, "tomorrow, we're going to work so damned hard we'll shift every bit of rock Gilbert blew up today. And if we unearth that gold that's supposed to be buried under the hill, then our chance will come. You ever seen what gold can do to men, Damiani?"

Damiani worked his feet under him and pulled himself upright. He strained on the chain, cursing all the time he tried to free himself. Failing, he turned on Blake Durant again.

"You tame me, Durant?" he asked hotly. "You, a damned drifter, Johnny-come-lately loner, going no place but into corners where folks can't see you proper. You, mister, tame me?" Damiani threw back his head and laughed scornfully. "Oh, man, that sure musta been hot today up there when you was lickin' Hopgood's boots and makin' a real fool of Curly into the bargain."

"Bromage has thrown in with me, Damiani," said Blake, "and after tonight's sorry business, I expect Warlow will, too. The others will fall into line and you'll be left one-out."

Blake looked down the wall where a stern-faced Curly Bromage sat. "Right, Bromage …?"

Bromage stared past Durant to Damiani. A nerve jumped at his temple and his jaw locked. He did not answer for a long time and when he finally spoke, his voice carried only as far as Damiani.

"That's about it, Danny," he said. "I think Durant's got the right slant on things. I can't see it's any use pestering these scum for no result." He looked round at Blake and said, "We wait and make one big charge together, Durant. You and me, and anybody else who wants to get out of here no matter if it means getting killed trying."

Danny Damiani came down as far as the chain would allow him. But even so he was still a couple of yards from Blake Durant. His stare went from Durant to Bromage and he growled, "Curly, if we get out of here, you ride a trail different to mine, you hear. By hell, if I get a noseful of your stink, I'll kill you."

Curly Bromage said nothing. He watched May Soncum moving away from Damiani, and saw Damiani's resentment increase. He knew that finally it would be a showdown between Damiani and Durant, and he was confused as to where his loyalty lay. Danny Damiani had saved his life twice, but against that he firmly believed that Durant, in his cool, calculating way, was smarter than Damiani, and if anybody could worm his way out of this hellhole, Durant would find the way.

Damiani, seeing May back away, glared furiously at Durant. The hatred in his eyes showed up plainly under the wash of moonlight.

"I'm going to kill you, Durant... kill you for sure," he whispered harshly across the silence of the night.

Blake Durant settled back as comfortably as he could and closed his eyes. He pushed all thought of this place from his mind and pulled on the memories of better places and better times. He knew he was right, just as he knew that if he failed he would be branded by Danny Damiani, and perhaps by all the rest of the men, as a coward.

The odds against success were suddenly so overwhelmingly strong, that he felt a chill run down his spine.

* * *

Bart Gilbert watched Will Hopgood drink from the neck of the whisky bottle while the other four guards came up behind him. There was a smell of rain in the air and he was certain the night had cooled suddenly and positively.

When Hopgood wiped his mouth on his sleeve and studied him grimly, Gilbert said, "You got three more bottles, Will. Where did you put them?"

Hopgood's brow creased into a frown and his stare narrowed. "Who said, Bart?"

"You have or you haven't, Will?" Gilbert pushed at him.

Hopgood straightened back from the table's edge and picked up his tobacco pouch. "If I tell you I ain't got no more, Bart, what then?"

Gilbert's face paled a little and his lips tightened. "Guess I'd have to believe you, Will. Only Berry just now said—"

"Berry talks a lot of loose hogwash, Bart. You believe him or me?"

Bart Gilbert looked sideways and saw two of the guards looking as worried as himself. "Guess I'd believe you, Will," he said.

"Fine," Hopgood growled, then he laughed and said, "So why don't you get the other bottles from behind the curtain? Hand them round, Bart, and let the men enjoy themselves."

Hopgood grinned widely, looking plainly very pleased with himself. Bart Gilbert fetched the bottles, took one himself and began to drink. When he felt the strong whisky burning his insides, he put down the bottle and wiped the neck on his grimy sleeve.

He glanced at Hopgood with a puzzled expression, muttered, "What the hell were you trying to find out just then, Will? Hell, why pester me with that kind of stuff? It's you and me, ain't it always been that way?"

"Might have been some changes, Bart," Hopgood said. "That Berry, he's a real fine talker, ain't he? For mine, he's been doing some riding high which I'm getting sick of. Feed them fools in the stockade, guard them every damn day, find that gold and then we'll split it up, man for man."

Hopgood drank again and leaned forward, his face twisting under a rise of bitterness. "Only, Bart, I got the feeling that Berry ain't going to play it fair. Why'd he send you here just now to check me out about that whisky? He wants us maybe to get at each other's throats now we're so close to getting our hands on that gold, eh? While we fight each other, keep tab on each other, what's he do, but sit in the shade, all the provisions in his keeping, the women bowing and scraping to him because he'd a dude big man, gives all the orders, makes all the plans." Hopgood's look swung onto the other four. They had come into the room and were seated against the wall on the bunk, handing the other two bottles around. "What about you four?" he said loudly. "You dumb or something?"

It was suddenly plain to Bart Gilbert that the whisky was having its effect on Will Hopgood. He had seen drink get the better of Hopgood before and seen a saloon near brought to the ground in the ruckus that followed. He wanted no part of any affair like that again. He turned to the others. "Well, what about it? You heard Will, didn't you?"

The four guards exchanged worried looks before one of them, a man called Jake Shepherd, said, "We ain't dumb, Hopgood."

"Then who're you backin'?" growled Hopgood. "Berry or me?"

Shepherd shifted his glass about on the window sill, and kept his gaze on the floor. Outside he could hear some of the saloon women chatting. With the whisky inside him and the day's work done, he wanted to do nothing but cut one of the women out of the crowd and go enjoy himself. Certainly, he told himself, he wanted no part of Will Hopgood in this mood.

"Didn't figure it come to backing anybody, Hopgood," he said. "Figured we was all in this together. We got those prisoners doing all the hard work for us, and the gold's close to being found, ain't it?"

"Bart says we'll see it tomorrow evening," Hopgood told him, ignoring a frown from Bart Gilbert as he spoke the lie.

Shepherd looked surprised. "That so? So soon?"

"Before the rains come, yeah," Hopgood went on. He stood up, swayed a little and pushed his hip against the table to keep himself steady. He grinned broadly and said, "Before the rains. Which means this time tomorrow night we're going to have our hands on a fortune. Now, what're we going to do about that? Some of you have got ties with the women. Maybe you got plans for the future with them, like taking your share and getting to hell outa here with them. Only it ain't goin' to be that way, I'm telling you now. The women will be shipped out in the morning and as soon as the gold is brought back here, it'll go into Berry's house. From there, who the hell knows what'll happen to it, or what'll happen to each of us."

The guards exchanged worried looks. Jake Shepherd came forward, looking fiercely belligerent. A small man, he nevertheless made a picture of somebody who had not bowed to many in his life. He said, sourly, "What're you getting at, Hopgood? What do you know that we don't?"

Hopgood leered at him. "You want to know, Shepherd?" he asked.

"I just asked you, didn't I?"

"Sure, you did." Hopgood took Shepherd by the shirt and wheeled him into the wall. "Mister, what I know is Berry's planning to run out on all of us. That's why we've got the likker tonight, and why he sent Bart here to check on what I was doing with it. He wants us snapping at each other's throats, so he can sit back and reap the rewards later. So something's got to be done about it, ain't it?"

"If it's true," Shepherd said tightly.

Hopgood's eyes blazed. "It's true, damn you! You callin' me a liar, mister?"

Shepherd shook his head in quick denial of this. "No, Hopgood, I know better than that. You're top gun here, and you don't have to prove it by pushing anybody about. If you know for sure Berry's planning to run out on us, then we best do something about it."

"Like?" Hopgood asked him.

"Like going, all of us," said Shepherd, "and putting it on the line to him. By hell, I haven't wasted three weeks in this hellhole for nothing. I signed up for my share of that gold and I'm going to get it."

Hopgood shoved him roughly back against the wall. "Wrong, Shepherd. You ain't goin' no place. What you're going to do, and the rest of you, too, is stay here and wait for me. None of you leave this building, no matter what happens. Got it?"

Shepherd looked anxiously Bart Gilbert's way. Gilbert was frowning and clearly unsure of himself. But when he said nothing, Shepherd picked up a bottle and drank. He turned his back on Will Hopgood and ignored him as Hopgood, staggering slightly, made for the door. In the doorway, Hopgood hesitated, muttered something under his breath to Bart Gilbert and then went off into the night.

* * *

Torp Berry was waiting on the porch, sitting in the dark, watching the clearing between his house and the guards' quarters. When he saw Will Hopgood stagger out across the porch, he smiled to himself. Then, very slowly, he drew his gun and put it on his lap. He lifted his legs and planted them on the porch rail and watched Hopgood come slowly across the clearing.

Will Hopgood, looking at the lighted windows at the end of the verandah, did not see Berry until he was on the porch itself. Then he stopped dead, surprised by the shape of the man in the porch chair.

Berry said, "Keep coming, Will. Got something on your mind?"

Hopgood cursed himself for a careless fool, but soon regained his composure. "Got plenty on my mind, Torp," he said easily. "Reckon you're going to double-cross me soon as you can. Tomorrow maybe."

"Didn't have that in mind, Will," Berry said. "Not that soon, anyway."

It took several seconds for the import of this to reach into Hopgood's drink-sodden mind. When it did, he straightened tall, and his hand slid down towards his gun butt. When Berry made no move to go for his gun, Hopgood slowly drew his gun. He felt uneasy, but he was determined to go through with what he had in mind by coming here.

"Not so soon?" he asked.

"Nope, Will," said Berry. "At the end of the week maybe, yeah. But not before I'd got rid of your women friends and not before all that treasure was stacked up where I could keep an eye on it. Then I guess I'd just kill you, Will, for the nuisance you've become, for the troublemaker you've become, for the damned fool you've become."

Hopgood was completely taken aback by what he considered was Torp Berry's gall. His grip on his gun tightened, but something stopped him from punching off a shot. He didn't understand that hesitation itself, unless it was that Torp Berry's confident tone suggested the boss man was not in the peril Hopgood thought him to be.

"And while we're at it, Will," Berry went on, "how about letting me know who else is in this with you? Gilbert? Shepherd? Ogilvie? O'Shea?"

"Everybody, damn you, Torp," Hopgood said. He worked the gun up in front of his gun belt where Torp Berry could see it plainly. "All the boys. They've decided to follow me now. The women ain't goin' no place and that gold will be divided fair. Then I'm going to get rid of all those fool prisoners and take the Soncum girl with me. How do you like the sound of that, Torp?"

"I don't like the sound of it at all, Will," Berry told him. "No, sir, not at all. The pity is, Will, for you, it's not going to happen that way."

Berry's gun exploded on his lap. The first echo of the shot had scarcely rung into the air when a second followed it. Then a third. Will Hopgood was thrown back onto his heels, then knocked to the side and the third bullet ripped through his forehead. He grabbed at the overhang post, made contact, and for a short moment hung there, with blood running down his forehead to blind him.

He made some grunting noises, then his grip lost its firmness and he pitched sideways to land heavily in the yard.

When he did not move, Berry rose from the chair and walked across to him. He turned him over with his boot as five men came charging out of the guards' quarters. Berry slipped back into the darkness along the rail and watched Bart Gilbert come running across the yard in full stride until he reached the halfway point where he suddenly slowed to a walk.

"Will? Will, you all right?" he called out.

Berry refilled his gun and waited for Gilbert to come on. He could at any moment have shot the guard down. But he enjoyed the spectacle of Gilbert's confusion so much that he held his fire. Gilbert saw the dark form lying on the ground and came forward at a run again. He went down beside the body and gasped when he recognized the face of Hopgood.

"Will, what the hell?" he muttered.

Torp Berry stepped into sight after checking to see that the other two guards had stayed back across the yard. He levelled his gun on Bart Gilbert and said very quietly, "Looking for somebody to be lying there instead of Hopgood, Bart?"

Gilbert came to his feet so rapidly that he almost toppled backwards.

He saw the gun and immediately shook his head. "Hell, Torp, I was just checking out the shooting, didn't know what the hell had happened. Will was drunk and talking a lot of nonsense. We couldn't shut him up. We figured, all of us, that—"

"What you should have done, Bart, was stop him," Torp Berry said and fired two shots into the lean gun hand.

Gilbert was hurled to the side, tripped over Hopgood's body and went down screaming in fright and pain. He lay writhing for a moment, then his body arched convulsively before he slumped down on the ground, lifeless.

Shepherd and O'Shea came forward into the pale moonlight, guns left in their holsters. They checked on Gilbert and Hopgood for a moment before Shepherd asked, "Want them buried, Torp?"

Torp Berry turned his smoking gun onto them. His face was tight with suspicion. He studied them bleakly for a long moment before he said, "What about the rest of you?"

"We signed on with you, Torp," Shepherd said. "Don't see there's anything happened to change that."

"O'Shea?" Berry growled.

"Same for me, Torp," said the other man quickly. "I got a stake in some gold and I figure you'll share even."

"I will."

"Then," O'Shea said, catching the lifeless Will Hopgood by the collar, "we best get rid of these fools. Too much drink, I reckon, turns a man's head, can stop his heart beating."

Shepherd dragged Bart Gilbert away while Torp Berry went back to the porch and called out to the two wall guards to continue their beat about the stockade. He slumped down into his porch chair and pushed fresh shells into his gun chamber. When he closed the chamber and returned the gun to its holster, he picked up his glass of whisky from behind the chair leg. Drinking it down in one gulp, he sighed out his satisfaction and reached for the bottle on the other side of the chair for a refill.

* * *

"Mr. Durant?"

Blake Durant had not slept a wink. He had sat there, letting his body relax and listening to the stamp of the guards' feet outside and to the two bursts of gunfire that had split the night's silence. He had seen May Soncum firstly take a position away from Danny Damiani, and then noticed that she ignored three later calls from Damiani. Since the last call, Damiani had been silent.

"Yeah, Miss Soncum?"

"Can I talk to you, Mr. Durant?"

"Why not?"

May joined him and after making sure she remained out of arm's reach, she sat down, carefully smoothed out her skirt, and studied him speculatively.

"Is it true what you said about the other men following you, Mr. Durant, and not Mr. Damiani?"

"It's true."

"But why? From the very moment you men arrived, all I've heard is Mr. Damiani speaking up. I don't recollect hearing you say anything. And by the look of you, you have suffered no hardship while Mr. Damiani has been whipped, brutally beaten up. Surely a leader of men should take some risks."

"He should when the time warrants it, Miss Soncum. What did you want exactly?"

May looked upwards at the high wall and was thoughtfully silent for a time. Then she answered, "What did you make of that shooting, Mr. Durant?"

"Nothing."

"Nothing at all? Can't you venture a guess?"

Durant shrugged. "Maybe a drunk letting off steam."

"No," May argued. "Surely you heard the cursing and that man screaming in pain."

Blake turned so he could see her better. The moonlight was washing over her, illuminating the loveliness of her features. He decided she was a disturbingly attractive young woman, and had it in his mind not to be so critical of Danny Damiani for mauling her.

"Yeah, I heard all that, Miss Soncum," he said finally, "but I don't know any more than you do what it was all about. Somebody got shot, but it wasn't one of us, was it?"

May frowned at him. "It doesn't bother you at all that a man has been killed. Are you that cold-hearted?"

"Are you worried, Miss Soncum, after what they did to you? Is there any one of those scum you have feeling for?" May blushed and then became suddenly angry. "I have no feeling but hate for them, Mr. Durant. Of that you may be sure. Given the chance I would kill them myself."

"Then settle back and relax for now, Miss Soncum," Blake told her. "It's going to be a long night and a worse day tomorrow than today was."

May looked suddenly disappointed but even as she rose to her feet again, pulling his range coat tighter about her body, she asked, "Will something happen to get us out of here? Have you really got a plan?"

"I'm working on it, Miss Soncum. You want some bolstering. Okay, I'll help you all I can. Stay away from Damiani and the rest of the men. We have troubles enough. When we make a move, if we do, go to ground and stay there, unless you're willing to help by distracting the guards when the opportunity presents itself."

"Distracting?" May asked him. "But how?"

Blake held her look evenly for a time. "You're a woman, Miss Soncum, and a lovely one at that. I haven't seen the women they've been playing about with but I know the kind who would come out here. So I'm sure a lot of those guards would be having thoughts about you. It's a lonely place for men."

May stepped back from him, a rise of horror showing in her face. "You mean you want me to... to ..." Her voice trailed off and she stood there, shocked speechless.

Blake Durant muttered, "Like I said, Miss Soncum, we're going to need all the breaks to get ourselves out of here. I think it will be tomorrow, late in the afternoon. Do what you like, but don't make things worse for us by tying up with Damiani."

Blake turned away and put his cheek against the rough, mud-covered wall.

He was aware that she had not moved away, but his body was still crying out for rest, so he closed his eyes and began to breathe evenly. Then he heard her going and he counted her steps until he knew she had returned to Damiani. Then he folded his arms about his broad, deep chest and pushed all thoughts of her from his mind.

CHAPTER SEVEN
Time for Dying

When the gate swung back, Blake Durant was standing at the head of the line. Curly Bromage was behind him. Then came Josh Warlow and a straggled line of men which ended with Danny Damiani standing off from the others with May Soncum alongside him. Damiani's face was bruised badly and his lips swollen. Yet when he looked at Torp Berry it was with undiminished defiance.

Berry moved with his usual relaxed walk down to the middle of the line and smiled easily. "Men, last night a couple of things happened that you should know about. Firstly, your old friend, Will Hopgood, got drunk and attacked me. I killed him."

The men exchanged disbelieving looks which made Berry smile wider.

"It's true," he told them. "Gilbert threw in his lot with Hopgood and naturally I had to kill him, too. I'm telling you this because I feel a few of you will be relieved that Will won't be wielding his whip any more. But I'm also telling you this because I want you to know that the beginning of the blood-shedding has begun. It will continue if any of you try to escape or cause trouble today. We're going out there to get the gold buried under the hill you've been working on."

Berry went on, "when I get my hands on that gold, I'm going to pack it into two wagons I have waiting. Then I'm going to take my men and get to hell out of here. I don't want to make things any more miserable for you than I have to, so get your heads down today and work hard. I must have that gold before the storms come, which I've been told should be any day now. If that happens before I get the gold, I will kill every one of you standing up in his boots."

The line of prisoners remained tensely silent. Berry moved back to the top of the line and waved to Shepherd to take the men through the gate. He then fell in behind Danny Damiani and spoke as he walked, "As for you, Damiani, I've got some real cute plans for you. The way I've heard it, you've been one real big headache from the time you got here. That hasn't been smart and unless you change your ideas, I'm going to cripple you for life and leave you to rot out here."

May Soncum, who had trailed along after the line of prisoners, threw a vicious look Berry's way. "You're mad," she said. "You're a loco killer!"

"Maybe I am, ma'am, and maybe I'm not," Berry said coldly. "But I hold all the trump cards and while I do, shut your damn mouth. I've heard enough from you, enough to last me a lifetime."

May opened her mouth to argue back, but Damiani dropped a hand on her arm and shook his head at her. May, lips pressed tightly together, went on, staring defiantly ahead.

The line made its way across the clearing and into the flat country and for the next hour the only sound in this forlorn part of the country was the steady tramp of boots across hard ground.

Finally they reached the hill and Blake Durant went straight to the equipment pile and pulled out the iron bar he had used the previous day. He winced as the weight of it pulled on the torn skin of his palms. But he was soon walking strongly ahead, and began his climb.

Berry shouted, "Not so fast, Durant. Hold it there." Blake stopped and peered back at him. Berry sent Shepherd to join him and while the other guards took their positions along the slopes, Berry settled down halfway up it, and perched himself on a tree stump.

"Durant," he called out loudly. "You're not fooling anybody. I've worked you out, mister, and feel I should tell you, I'm not being taken in by your show of submission. I don't know what the hell you were before you came here but I know what Bromage was. He's taking advice from you, and that suits me fine. But don't expect things to break your way, Durant. The only thing that will break here is your blasted neck if you worry me. Now get to work and shift that hill."

Blake Durant looked across to where Curly Bromage was already trying to dislodge a huge boulder. He went across to Bromage and when Shepherd moved away to take a position on the higher ground, Blake dug his bar deep under the boulder and said quietly, "We'll move at noon. I don't think many of the men can take much more after then."

"Suits me," Bromage said. "But what if we get out of here... cut down a few of these scum... what about the gold?"

Blake grunted as he exerted himself to shift the boulder. Rubble spilled away from below him. He dug his heels in deeper and his shoulder and back muscles bulged.

"I doubt if it's here," Blake said.

Bromage frowned at him. "How come?" he asked.

Blake shrugged. "I've travelled a lot, Bromage, and I've heard a heap of stories about hidden gold. I've seen men kill for a map which could not lead them anywhere but to Boothill. Maybe there is gold, maybe there isn't. But for now, forget about it. When the time comes, take Shepherd. I'll handle Berry."

Curly Bromage spat on his hands and took a firmer grip on his bar. Using all his strength he helped Durant shift the boulder and sent it rolling.

Below them, smoking quietly, his stare constantly searching, Torp Berry grunted his satisfaction. And just away from him, working with Josh Warlow, Danny Damiani scowled in the direction of Durant and Bromage. The rest of the men, under instructions from O'Shea, were clearing the rubble and uprooted tree stumps from the bottom of the slope to let the big boulders roll away onto the flat country.

The sun rose and brilliant yellow sunlight filled the section. The heat gradually became more intense until every man working on that slope was bathed in sweat. But Torp Berry merely sat and watched, aware that with the increase in the day's heat, an increase of hatred towards him was rising, too. He could not have cared less, as he counted off the minutes which were taking him closer to a fortune.

* * *

"How about a drink, Berry?" Danny Damiani asked in mid-morning and Berry answered with a shake of his head and a crooked smile.

Damiani threw down his iron bar and faced him squarely. "I can't swallow, damn you. How can you expect a man to work if he can't hardly breathe?"

"The others are managing, Damiani," said Berry. "If the dust worries you, get up higher with Bromage and Durant. I reckon the three of you should work together anyway, three big men, three men who run this outfit of fools, don't you?"

Danny Damiani glared furiously at him and picked up his bar again. But instead of moving to higher ground he glared at Durant and Bromage and bent to work again.

Another hour went by before Josh Warlow fell to the ground exhausted.

O'Shea crossed to him and kicked him to his feet again, but seeing the glazed look in Warlow's eyes, he hurried back to consult with Torp Berry. Berry, after a long contemplation of Warlow's condition, told O'Shea to give the old-timer a drink.

Danny Damiani waited for Warlow to lift the canteen to his parched lips before he suddenly threw himself at Warlow and wrenched the canteen away. Before O'Shea could stop him, he was pouring water down his throat and spilling a great deal down his shirt.

O'Shea grabbed him, hurled him to the ground and kicked him in the jaw. Damiani gave a grunt and rolled away and O'Shea picked up the canteen. Warlow came with outstretched hands to get a drink, but O'Shea, sullen now, pushed him back down the slope.

Torp Berry came hurrying up and laid his gun butt across Damiani's head and sent him rolling to the bottom of the slope. All the prisoners had ceased work and were regarding a distraught Warlow pityingly as the old man begged for a drink.

But Torp Berry merely brushed him aside saying, "You had your chance, Warlow. Too bad you missed it."

"I'll die, damn you, Berry," Warlow insisted and for this he got a blow on the shoulders from O'Shea which sent him toppling down to join the unconscious Danny Damiani.

Blake Durant watched this incident coolly until Bromage asked, "Now, Durant?"

"Not yet."

"But why in hell?"

"Berry's playing out a game, Bromage," Blake said. "And there can only be one winner and one loser. So far the loser is Damiani, curse him!"

"Blasted fool," Bromage agreed. "But, damn him, he's got guts to burn."

"He's got that," Blake said and moved to higher ground to dislodge another rock. Suddenly his feet went from under him and he went down in a shower of dust. The boulder he had just got moving gathered speed and raced away down the slope to bounce over those already there and race out onto the flat empty country.

Torp Berry was quickly at Blake's side, digging his gun into his back and forcing him to his feet and then away from the hole gaping up at the three of them.

Berry's face brightened and he peered into the hole excitedly, finally saying, "There it is! It's here!"

O'Shea, Shepherd and two other guards came running up towards them. Blake Durant picked up his iron bar and braced himself. He gave Curly Bromage a terse nod and then swung the iron bar with all his remaining strength.

The bar smacked into O'Shea's middle and sent him hurtling down the slope. Curly Bromage immediately charged at Shepherd and managed to land one solid punch on the smaller man's jaw before Torp Berry called out wildly, "Hold it, Bromage! Durant, damn you!"

Curly Bromage hesitated only long enough to see Blake Durant grabbing up O'Shea's gun. He dived for Shepherd's gun but a bullet smacked into his wrist and he let out a grunt of pain and drew back. Dust was thick now.

Durant called out loudly, "Keep going, Bromage. This is it! All or nothing!"

Bromage didn't wait for more. A second shot tore a gash along his jaw but he paid the injury no heed as he hurdled over a rising Shepherd and put his knee into the man's face. Shepherd went down moaning, as Bromage went on. Out of the thick screen of dust he saw Blake Durant pulling Josh Warlow to his feet. Bromage went down towards Danny Damiani. But he had just begun to haul a still stunned Damiani to his feet when rifle fire burst all about them.

Blake Durant said, "Josh, get the men back to the water tower and keep them there. Bromage, get to Berry's place, find what guns you can and take them to the tower."

"What about Danny?" Bromage asked, and Blake saw a genuine worry reach into the big man's face.

"Up to you," he said. "For mine the others are more important. Get control of the water and the rest will sort itself out."

Blake felt a twinge of pain along the top of his shoulder but just then he saw May Soncum running for her life from one of the guards. He punched off a shot and the guard went down. Blake made for him, picked up his rifle and then grabbed May Soncum by the arm and pulled her into the brush.

Prisoners were running everywhere and although Blake kept yelling for them to make for the tower a lot of them ran wildly in the other direction. Feeling he had done all he could here, Blake hurried along, making his own trail through the dense dry brush. His lungs were bursting when he finally stopped and May Soncum collapsed on the ground at his feet.

She looked up distraughtly at him and moaned, "I can't go on. I can't, Mr. Durant!"

"You've got to. Take a minute's rest then get to the tower. Once you're there, get Bromage to look after things."

"What are you going to do?" May asked him anxiously.

"I'm not sure," he said.

Bromage, dragging a limp and stunned Damiani with him, suddenly burst through the brush. Blake pushed the six-gun into Bromage's fist and told him to go on. He then walked carefully back into the break of the brush and took cover behind a tree.

May Soncum struggled to her feet, amazed at this big man's endurance. She had seen the whole affair from the very beginning and knew the risks Durant had taken. It seemed to her now that everything he had done, was to help somebody else; Even his killing of the guard who had almost caught her, proved that he had no regard for his own safety. She felt a warmth creeping into her.

Then he was gone, and Bromage was urging her to hurry. She hesitated, still watching Blake Durant. Then she saw him go down on one knee and heard his rifle blasting.

With a cry she broke into a stumbling run and followed Bromage and Damiani back along the dusty trail.

* * *

Torp Berry pulled a doubled-over O'Shea to his feet and slammed him back against a boulder's edge.

"Come on, damn you, we've got to get them," he snarled. "You ain't anythin' but winded, you damn fool!"

But although he tried to straighten, O'Shea's face filled with agonized pain.

"Got somethin' busted inside," he said. Shepherd rose up beside him, studied him grimly and shook his head at Berry. Berry grunted and pushed O'Shea away, picked up his own gun and went scrambling down the slope. At the bottom he found one of the guards dead and the others gone through the brush.

Calling to Shepherd he gave chase and came up a hundred yards further on to find two guards standing off from a break in thicker brush. Rifle fire was keeping the guards pinned down.

Berry, yelling wildly, charged forward. A rifle blast knocked him off his feet and he rolled along the ground for several yards before, partly dazed, he came to a halt alongside a deadfall log. He sat up, felt his head and smeared blood down his shirt. Shepherd reached him and dropped down beside him.

Berry, scowling blackly, growled, "I'm not hurt much. Get those others up here. I seen Durant. By hell, I want his hide, I want him bad."

Shepherd called the others up. The rifle fire had stopped. He listened above the settling silence and told Berry, "He's gone on, I think. What now?"

"Get after him, damn you, what else? Those scum haven't got but two guns between them and I hid all the other guns when Hopgood was double-crossing me. They won't find them. Keep at them until they exhaust all their shots. Then, by hell, we're going to have ourselves a real massacre."

Shepherd went off on the run straight into the brush opening. But as soon as he cleared the opening, a last shot from Blake Durant tore one of his kneecaps open. He went down on his face and the rest of the guards who were following him through halted and went to ground.

Torp Berry, wiping blood from his face and trying to work out the extent of his injury with probing fingers, came walking up behind them. He looked angrily down at the uplifted faces and then stared ahead.

But the whole section was quiet again. Shepherd struggled to his feet, inspected his knee and tore a strip from his shirt. He bandaged the wound and limped into shade. O'Shea came up still doubled over and coughing up blood, and Torp Berry, after a string of curses had been hurled at his remaining men, leaned against a tree stump and did some thinking.

CHAPTER EIGHT
Fight for Survival

Blake Durant was almost out on his feet when he walked into the clearing between the two houses. The sun streamed down on him and dried the sweat almost before it formed. He felt as if he could lie down and sleep for a year.

Josh Warlow was standing outside the smaller of the two houses drinking from a canteen. When he saw Durant he called out, "The women have bolted, Durant. Looks like they left in two wagons, heading west."

Blake nodded, crossed to Warlow and accepted the canteen from him. After quenching his thirst, he leaned against the porch overhang post and stared in the direction he had just come. "What about the others?" he asked.

"Bromage got most of them under the tower. Then he went looking for guns. Damiani's hurt bad, but conscious again. By hell, he takes some stopping, don't he?"

"He's a damned fool!" Blake exploded and pushed himself upright again.

Warlow let it go at that, seeing the weariness in Durant's face and feeling the big man had done enough for all of them for the moment, not to be worried by senseless talk. "Miss Soncum?" Blake asked.

"Looking after Damiani," Warlow told him and noticed a slight pucker reach into Durant's brow before Durant left the porch and made for the water tower. Warlow followed him but they were still a hundred yards short of the structure when Berry, Shepherd, a limping O'Shea and two other guards came into the end of the clearing.

Blake Durant told Warlow to go on, dropped to the ground and fired carefully at the oncoming bunch of armed men. He saw one man go down and two others trip over him. Then Berry broke away to the cover of the side of the smaller house and Shepherd went with him.

Blake got to his feet, wondering how much further he could go on, and dragged himself towards the tower. Warlow was waiting outside the structure, looking worried.

Warlow, in answer to Blake's questioning frown, pointed inside the tower structure and said, "Damiani."

Blake brushed Warlow aside and ducked in under some crossbeams to find seven prisoners huddled in the dimness, with May Soncum sitting against a solid tower post and Damiani, grinning, holding a gun.

Blake snapped, "What are you up to now, Damiani?"

Damiani raised the gun level with Blake's stomach, and said, "Taking over, Durant. I'm obliged for what you've done this far, but sitting here I got to thinking. This is gun country again, ain't it? And like Curly likely told you, gun country is where I get to be top man. I'll have that rifle, pronto."

"Go to hell!" Blake told him.

Damiani snagged back the hammer of the gun and leered up at Blake. "I ain't sayin' it again, Durant. Give me the gun."

Warlow pushed forward, seething with anger. "By hell, Damiani, ain't you got no brains at all? Berry's still out there and closing in fast. No sense at all in us fighting each other. We got the water and Curly'll get us some more guns. What we're up against is Berry and his bunch of killers."

"What we're up against, Warlow," snapped Damiani, "is your fool talk. Sit down now. Berry found his gold, or better, Durant found it for him, so he ain't goin' to be worried about us so much, not till he digs it out. By then we'll be fed, have all the water we want and maybe have some guns. But till we do, damn you, I'm in charge. What I say goes."

"What the hell does it matter?" Warlow said sharply.

Damiani's eyes went black with anger. "It matters. Durant knows it does. No more talk now. Durant, it'll take you too long to reload even if you had fresh shells. I been listenin' to that rifle go off. Be empty by now, mister. Right?"

Blake's lips thinned. He stole a look at May Soncum and found her looking terribly worried. The other men all seemed to be concerned, too.

But since Damiani had the gun, he knew they could do nothing. It seemed to him then that there was only one thing to do, and that was to bow to Damiani's senseless dictate and wait for Curly Bromage to show his hand.

What Bromage would do, with all that gold within easy reach, Blake was no longer sure. Bromage had risked his life getting Damiani out of the gunfire thrown at them by Berry's outfit. So how far did his loyalty to Damiani really reach?

He tossed the rifle to Damiani and said, "If there'd been a shell in it, Damiani, I'd have killed you."

With that, and with Damiani's scornful laughter lifting from the bottom of the tower structure, Blake Durant went out into the sunlight again.

* * *

Torp Berry was worried. Standing in the shade of the house wall, he watched Shepherd getting his knee bandaged. O'Shea was doubled over against the wall, his face as white as parchment. Berry realized that neither of them would be much good to him in a tough fight like the one he expected lay ahead of them.

So he worked out his strength without them. Three guards, and himself. Against him he had Durant, Damiani, Warlow, Bromage and a crowd of jaspers who would be more liability to Durant than a help. Then there was the girl, who would also be a burden, too.

He looked up at the sky to find it cloudless. Where previously that clear sky would have made him happier in mind, now it worried him deeply. There was no water but what was in the tower and he saw now that Durant, sensibly, had decided to make a stand under it.

Looking about with deeper resentment at his men, he growled, "We got to take that tower. They've only got two guns and no supply of shells. So spread out and keep putting shots under the tower. Sooner or later they'll break."

The guards quickly moved away and Torp Berry, shoving his own gun back into its holster, went across to Shepherd. He had little time for any of these men, but Shepherd had proved himself reliable and obedient thus far. And he needed somebody to run one flank while he ran the other. He said, "How bad is it?"

"Hurts like blazes, Torp."

"Reckon it should. But can you move about? Hell, we've got a couple of hours to go through, then we'll come out on top again. That'll mean gold, water, food, horses, any damn thing we want. You got to get on your feet and help in this fight. The others might decide to call it a day."

"They've come this far," Shepherd muttered, but Torp Berry merely gave a grunt and answered:

"So did Gilbert and Hopgood, near this far anyway. And you seen what got into them, Shepherd. No, I got to have you on your feet. Here, let me have a look at that."

Berry bent down and pulled the bandage pad away from the knee wound. He winced when he saw the jagged edges of bone sticking through the torn flesh.

"Don't look too bad," he lied. "Let's see if you can get up. Better to have weight on it, send it numb. You lie down, mister, you ain't ever going to get up."

Shepherd studied him grimly while Berry forced his hand under his armpit. Biting his lip against the drive of expected pain, Shepherd then hauled himself to his feet. A low groan of pain escaped through his white lips and sweat ran down both sides of his face.

"See now," Berry said. "Ain't so bad, is it?"

"It hurts like all crazy, Torp," Shepherd said and his body quivered as pain wracked it.

Berry held onto him for a moment longer but when Shepherd began to go limp in his grip, his eyes closing, he suddenly shoved him away brutally and growled, "Damn you, you're like the rest. A little pain and you throw up. To hell with you then. Lie down and die!"

Torp Berry snatched Shepherd's gun from his hand and pushed it into his gun belt. Shepherd fell and lay motionless on the ground. The only sign that life still worked through him came from the deep groans that shook his body.

Berry left him and worked his way down the side wall. Reaching the back as gunfire broke out all about him, he saw splinters of timber flying off the tower's supporting crossbeams. Heartened by this sight, he hurried to the other corner where he could see the whole clearing better. Two guards had positioned themselves so that they had two sides of the tower under surveillance. Their gunfire made such a racket that the whole place seemed about to explode in Berry's face.

Grinning, and becoming more confident by the minute, he broke into the open and made for the stockade wall. O'Shea and Ogilvie, a big, slow-moving man, saw him run and went after him.

When Berry stopped breathless against the wall, out of range of gunfire from the tower, he told them, "Hell, we got them beat already. They ain't got no bullets."

"Might be foxing," O'Shea said.

"Nope, they've played their hand. We got them. Move in."

O'Shea studied him grimly before he threw a worried look Ogilvie's way. Ogilvie shifted resentfully when Berry planted a hand on his back and pushed him forward. And when Ogilvie stopped, part-turning to check out O'Shea again, Berry snarled, "Move, damn you! Don't you think I know what I'm doing?"

Ogilvie scratched his jaw with the barrel of his rifle and still hesitated. Then O'Shea nodded at him and moved forward in a crouch. Together they went straight across the clearing and got to within twenty yards of the tower before a bullet took Ogilvie in the head. He went down without a sound and O'Shea, after blasting a round of shots into the tower structure, turned on his heels and fled.

Torp Berry broke into a wild fit of cursing and tried to gun him down. But this action instead of stopping O'Shea in his tracks, only served to alert the other two guards to Berry's madness. Slowly, furtively, they left their positions and went back to O'Shea and Shepherd.

At the last moment, Torp Berry saw the back of one of them disappearing behind the wall of the smaller ranch house. His gun lifted but he held his fire. Then, realizing what had happened, he broke from cover and ran as fast as he could for the house.

Two shots ripped through the air in front of his face, a third tore his shirt open and grazed his chest. In panic, he wheeled about and ran blindly in the other direction and when he reached the stockade wall again, he collapsed against it and moaned into his hands.

* * *

O'Shea said grimly, "He's loco. No mistake about it."

"Yeah," Shepherd agreed. "What d'you reckon to do from here?"

"Get to hell out of it," O'Shea said. He looked at the other two men and they nodded ready agreement to this.

Shepherd, helped to his feet by O'Shea, gritted his teeth against the pain in his leg and said with an air of authority, "Okay, we'll need horses. There's canteens back at the hill. It should be enough to get us back to Maple. We can work something else out once we get there."

"Suits me fine," O'Shea backed him up. "I need my head examined for being out here in the first place. I never did trust Hopgood and Berry's broken down. Let's go."

"I'll have to wait here," Shepherd told him. "I can't walk a step."

"You can ride though?" O'Shea asked him.

"I can start by trying, Larry," Shepherd said and sank against the wall. He held his side firmly, fighting down an urge to cry out as sharper pain worked upwards into his thigh.

O'Shea and the others went off through the timber of the slopes to fetch the horses and Shepherd clung to the wall, feeling his strength wasting away by the minute. Somehow, feeling the warmth of the sun lessening, he knew he would not make it.

* * *

Blake Durant met Curly Bromage on the porch of the big ranch house. Bromage looked savagely about him and kicked a chair off the porch. The legs broke as it went rolling out into the clearing.

"Not a damned gun any place," he growled. "Damn Berry, he musta hid them, expecting something like this to happen."

Blake heard him out before he went into the house. Bromage had pulled the place apart and the wreckage of his searching lay everywhere, making obstacles to Durant's progress through the rooms.

Joining Bromage five minutes later, he said, "We're wasting our time here. Berry wouldn't leave guns where any of his men could find them. But that's not my greatest worry right now, Bromage."

Bromage held his look evenly. "What is then, Durant? Hell, we got this far, we can make it further, can't we?"

"Maybe we can. Why did you give Damiani the gun?"

Bromage studied him heavily. "Why in hell not, he's one of us, isn't he? None of the others had a gun or anything to fight with. You said to hold onto the water tower so I gave the gun to Danny. He can use it fine, if that's what you're worrying about, Durant."

"I'm not doubting his ability, Bromage," Blake told him. "But I think I know why he wants it. He took my rifle, too. It was a matter of killing him, or bowing down to him."

Bromage's mouth gaped open. "He took the rifle? What in hell for? You and him, it's gone deeper, Durant?"

"It has."

Bromage spun about and slammed a fist at the porch overhang post. The whole porch rocked under the power of the blow. Then Bromage stormed off the porch and hurried towards the second house. But as he did so rifle fire slammed into the tower. A bullet hit the bottom of the tower tank itself and a spurt of water sprang out in an arc towards the ground. Bromage stopped dead in his tracks. Then, as a stray bullet sought him out he ducked back and returned to Blake Durant.

He had just struck the porch post in anger again when he saw Ogilvie and O'Shea run from the cover of the stockade wall. When Ogilvie went down and O'Shea retreated, Bromage said, "Like I said, Danny can use a gun. Let's go see him, Durant. I'm sure we can work this out."

Blake Durant looked dubiously at him, but stuck in the house, without arms, he decided he had no choice. They saw Berry try to cut across the clearing only to be forced back to the stockade wall and once he had gone from sight again, Durant and Bromage made a dash for the tower.

But this time no bullets followed them. Bromage was first to duck in under the crossbeams and went straight to Danny Damiani. He saw in one glance that Damiani had both the rifle and the six-gun.

His face scarlet with anger, he snapped, "What the hell, Danny? Damn you, you want to ruin everything now, when we got the drop on them? We stick together and we can blast our way out of here."

"We're going nowhere," Danny Damiani told him. "Not till we've got that gold. We worked hard enough for it, didn't we, got whipped, beaten up, were starved and left to die of thirst? I ain't leavin' without it."

Curly Bromage scowled blackly and leaned closer to him. "Danny, I've ridden through all kinds of hell with you, but I'm going no further while you talk like this. Forget the damned gold, likely it's not there anyway."

"Berry seen it," Damiani argued and looked furiously at Blake Durant as if defying him to say otherwise.

"He seen a hole, nothing else," Curly said. "And why shouldn't there be holes when Gilbert blasted half the hill away? I'm telling you, Danny, you're on your own if you go through with this. We got a heap of sick men on our hands and a woman to look after."

Damiani grinned crookedly at him and prodded his chest with the gun. "Curly, you look after these fool jaspers and I'll look after Miss Soncum. And I'll get me the gold and all you'll get is a pat on the back from Durant. The other way, you throw in with me and we get these fools to dig up that gold for us. Be about where they were before, won't it? So no harm done and we'll feed them, give them drink and not beat the stuffin' out of them. You and me, Curly, we can pull this off."

Blake Durant made a sudden move forward but Damiani lifted the gun and levelled it on him. His mouth twisted and his voice was a snarl when he said, "Durant, you do that. You do it and save me a lot of worry about you. What I want from you, mister, is the kind of hard work you did for Torp Berry. Nothing else."

Blake straightened. Josh Warlow worked himself onto his feet and said in a muffled tone, "Damiani, I think you been through too much. Hopgood hurt you more than you let on. Now hand over the gun and let's sit down and work a way out of this for all of us. I'm going along with Bromage and Durant."

Damiani slowly rose to his full height. His eyes were narrow and his face looked ugly under a mask of enveloping bitterness.

"Warlow, I told you once, shut down!" he snarled. "Durant, get over there with him. Miss Soncum, you get outside and when I say so, you run for the big house. We'll make our stand there and these fools can wait here for whatever's coming their way."

May Soncum stood up and looked keenly at Blake Durant. She was desperately weary and terribly confused. But in the back of her mind was the memory of the risks Blake Durant had taken for all of them. He should, she decided, be already dead.

Then to Damiani she said, "My father was a fool when it came to believing stories. It was he who brought the old map of that hill out here and showed it to Torp Berry. From the very beginning, Berry was skeptical of finding any gold at all, but as the days went by he became obsessed with the idea that my father had really happened onto a true story and a true map this once in his life. But if you ask me, and I lived twenty-four years with my father, he would never have found gold out here. He was not destined to ever find gold. He was that kind of unfortunate dreamer."

Damiani reached out and pulled her to him. "No lies," he barked. "I'm sick of damned lies, and sick of you not making up your mind about what side you're on. I run this show, I just told you, and if you want to get all the comforts you've dreamed about and me into the bargain, you just do as you're told. Now get outside and see what's happening. If you see anybody, just say the word."

May did not move. Damiani pushed her away and levelled the gun on her. But Curly Bromage suddenly sprang forward. He got his hand on Damiani's wrist and began to force the gun down. May Soncum screamed and backed away and the other prisoners, led by Josh Warlow, stormed forward to help Curly Bromage.

But before they could get close enough, the gun went off and Curly Bromage let out a cry.

His body was beginning to sag when Blake Durant hurled himself at the opening under the crossbeams and raced away from the tower structure. A bullet whipped after him but missed and he ran on through the noon heat, back to the main ranch house.

CHAPTER NINE
A Stockade Burns

"Curly, you all right? Damn you, say something."

Danny Damiani shook Curly Bromage roughly by the shoulder. Warlow and the other men, and May Soncum with them, had withdrawn to the other side of the tower. They stood there, closely bunched, watching a worried Danny Damiani beg his trail friend for a sound.

Bromage opened his eyes, gritted his teeth against a drive of pain and looked Damiani straight in the eyes. "Danny, you're loco," he said hoarsely. "You got the same fever Berry has."

"I got good common-sense, that's all," Damiani defended himself. "So don't you go fancy on me, Curly. It's you and me and we'll pull this off, you'll see."

Bromage shook his head and said nothing more. Damiani rose from his side and went to the crossbeams. He peered out into the noon heat and squinted to see past the shimmers and sun glare. Nothing moved and there was no sound. Then suddenly the day erupted with noise. Danny Damiani jerked upright and stared harder. The sound of hoofbeats rose above the day's deathly silence.

"They're pulling out!" he cried out. "We've licked 'em, Curly. You hear me, mister. We've won out!"

Curly Bromage still said nothing. None of the others moved but Josh Warlow muttered, "I think he's right. They've had enough maybe and decided to move on. Let's get to hell out of here."

"Everybody stays put," Damiani snarled, turning and levelling his gun on Warlow. "Nobody goes any place, unless I say so."

With that, he moved out through the beams and stood on the clearing with the sun full in his face, highlighting his bruises and swollen lips, gashed brows and straggled, grimy hair.

But just as suddenly as the hoofbeats had disrupted the day's silence, they died. Damiani scowled darkly across the clearing, and saw one horse making cover behind the other house. He lifted his gun, was tempted to fire off a shot, but thought better of it.

He tried to work out what they were up to, but his thoughts were confused. Durant had run for his life, cut out on them. He himself had a gun with one bullet left in it. One bullet, but he told himself he was still armed with a lot of bluff and soon he would get himself a gun belt and God help anybody who got in his hair then.

* * *

Larry O'Shea looked about this place which had known so many killings and would have more.

Then, with a resigned shrug, he muttered to himself, "I'm heading out. I only want to forget this place and forget the whole stinkin' mess."

Larry O'Shea went to his horse, swung tiredly up and looked off into the distance. Then without another word he put his horse into a run. He had just cleared the end of the house when a shot rang out through the noon's silence.

O'Shea pulled his horse up, turned it. Torp Berry, standing against the stockade wall and refilling his gun, glared insanely back at him.

O'Shea dug his heels in and put the horse into a run. A shot slammed into his shoulder and almost toppled him from the saddle. But he managed to pull himself upright, then drew his own gun and bore down on Torp Berry.

Berry, in sudden panic, realized that he was a perfect target for a killer, standing there with the sunlight beaming down on him. He dropped to the ground and punched off another four shots, but O'Shea kept coming. Berry, saliva running from his mouth, down his chin, rolled over twice as bullets cracked into the ground and the wall.

Then O'Shea, his face deadly white from the pain burning through him, mouth set so firmly that he seemed to have no lips, and his brows crowding his eyes almost out of sight, came thundering in.

"Your turn, Berry!" he called out hoarsely, but Torp Berry fired off one last desperate shot which smashed into O'Shea's face and sent him bucking from the horse.

O'Shea landed on his back, bounced once, his legs flying high, and landed with a thud on his side. He hung there for a moment before a grunt came out of him and he dropped onto his back and his lifeless face stared at the cloudless sky.

Danny Damiani watched the horse career by and swore violently because he knew he had no chance of reaching it. With a horse he could really be master of this situation.

Just as he was lamenting his lost opportunity, Blake Durant broke from the other house porch and went racing after the big black. The horse saw him and, wild-eyed, stepped up its pace until inexplicably it slewed about, pawed the air, then came to a halt with black sides heaving. Damiani saw Durant lift a hand and quieten the horse, then swing into the saddle and ride from sight.

Danny Damiani looked sidelong to find May Soncum frowning after the disappearing Blake Durant. For the first time he understood her real feelings towards Durant.

"Okay, now you seen that, didn't you, Miss Soncum?" said Damiani. "What've you got to say now about Durant and all his high talk?"

"You ready to trust him still when you seen him get a horse and beat it to hell outa here. I'm telling you, ma'am, Durant's a coward and when I catch up with him one day I'm going to make him answer for what he just done."

May's look clouded as she heard the hoofbeats die away. Suddenly a deep desperation took hold of her. She realized with a deep disappointment that she had put a lot of faith in Blake Durant. He had seemed to her to be the only one here who really thought things out. The others, and especially Danny Damiani, acted too rashly, reminding her of her father when he was alive.

Her shoulders slumped and she ducked under the crossbeams and crossed to the far wall. There she felt Warlow's look fixed on her while Curly Bromage studied her grimly.

"It was Mr. Durant," she explained. "He got a horse and rode out."

Warlow pinched his lips and Bromage sagged back and let out a gasp. When he closed his eyes, May realized that like herself, these two men had put all their faith in Blake Durant. And Durant had let them all down.

* * *

Torp Berry's mind worked feverishly. He realized he had been loco trying to get across the open country. So he went right around the high stockade wall until he reached the far side.

There he piled brush and small logs against the wall and started a fire. When the flames came, he fed more timber onto them until he had a fire roaring up the wall for ten feet or more. Then he hurriedly stacked more timber for yards along the wall towards the south where the wind was heading.

Standing back, he watched the fire take hold until the whole section was covered with black smoke. Satisfied the stockade would eventually burn to the ground and would take hours doing that, he made his way along the trail, heading for the hill Bart Gilbert had blasted for him.

He was careful when he got near it to check about him, with the thought in his mind that perhaps Shepherd had betrayed him and had brought the other guards here and they were at that moment loading his gold into saddlebags.

While this thought began to worry him more and more, Berry increased his pace. Never a person to exert himself too much, he soon found his feet aching badly.

But he kept going, with the sight of that big hole always in his mind. His gun was full, and he felt he could still beat the lot of them... Durant, Warlow, Bromage and Damiani, and his own men, too, if they'd turned against him. The gold... that was all that mattered.

The sun burned him and the heat sapped his strength. He began to stagger and his mind began to wander. He found himself thinking of the days back east when he had courted some of the most beautiful women in the towns he passed through. They had always given him a good reception at first, but always, too, money troubles had come to make him shift on.

He decided that one day, as soon as he got his gold, he would deck himself out in the finest clothes he could buy, get a good rig and return to spit in the faces of some of those snob-nosed women who had despised him. He would spit in the faces of a lot of men, too, who had expressed their scorn and distrust of him.

He went on with firmer tread until he sighted the first of the boulders Durant had prised clear of the slope. Reluctantly he was forced to admire Durant's strength and determination. He doubted if any other man in his knowledge could have worked under such difficulties as Durant and still kept his temper in check.

Then he was on the slope and found himself surprised at being there. He realized again that the heat was playing tricks on him. His sight was wavering, things were becoming indistinct.

He looked anxiously about him and the silence worried him. The wind was still coming across his face but although he could feel his hair blowing wildly, the wind did nothing to cool him down. He began talking to himself as he dragged himself up to the hole Durant had unearthed for him.

He climbed for ten minutes before he found himself on the very top of the slope. And he had missed the hole. He came down again but reached the bottom without finding it. He was exhausted now and he sat down and hugged his head between his knees. He forced himself to keep thinking. This was the hill... The hole was here... The gold was here...

He pushed himself to his feet and saw a big shape directly in front of him. Through his blurred vision, he made out the features of a man, the build of a very big man.

Torp Berry lifted his gun and tried to keep it steady. Then an explosion went off in his head and terrible pain blinded him. He pawed the air before crashing on his face.

He was sobbing when Blake Durant dragged him by the collar and took him off into the shade of the brush halfway up the rock-strewn slope.

* * *

Danny Damiani had made up his mind. There was one way to get the gold and that was to dig it out. He forced Warlow and the others outside the tower structure and kept May Soncum alongside him. His pains had all left his body and he felt suddenly very much alive.

"Okay, move out!" he told Warlow and the others.

"We're going for a little walk and do some work. And when that's over, you can all come back here and have all the grub you like, all the sleep you like and all the whisky you like. Me, I'll have moved on."

Curly Bromage stood against the latticework of the structure and eyed his one-time trail friend bitterly. His disappointment at Blake Durant having let them down had long since died.

Curly Bromage, who had been a loner until he had tied up with Danny Damiani, decided he was one again. He did not even care much what happened to Warlow or the others, or even much what happened to May Soncum. She was, he had finally decided, a young woman who could look after herself well enough.

"Danny, listen to me once more, will you?" he asked Damiani.

"Sure, Curly. Speak it out, but be fast about it. We got a lot of work to be done, but if you don't feel up to it, don't worry about it. I still got an opening for you in my outfit, only I ain't about to trust you until I've got everything I want from this caper."

Bromage held his stomach with his hand. A dull ache still pounded away inside his body but May Soncum had expertly dressed his wound, and he felt sure that, given plenty of rest, he would pull through.

"What if there is no gold, Danny?" Bromage put to him.

Danny Damiani wheeled on him, grabbing him by the shirt. "What if there is, damn you? That's what you got to think about, Curly. You say one more word like that and so help me I'll kill you. I mean it, mister, there's enough others to do the digging without I should have to worry about you."

Curly Bromage licked his lips and rocked back on his heels. "Forget it then, Danny," he said painfully and moved alongside Josh Warlow who put an arm under his armpit and helped him along.

Painfully and slowly the procession of men and one woman made its way through the day's intense heat. Even with Damiani urging them on all the time, it took them over an hour to reach the diggings. There they found the place just as they had left it so many trouble-packed hours earlier.

Damiani immediately sent Warlow to inspect the hole. Warlow labored up the slope and looked about for several minutes before he cupped his hands about his mouth and called down, "There isn't a hole here, Damiani."

"Don't he to me, mister," Damiani called out, pushing May Soncum roughly aside and striding forward angrily.

"I'm telling you, damn you, Damiani, I ain't blind," said Warlow. "There isn't a hole that I can see. Come look for yourself."

Damiani turned on the others. "Stay put," he snapped. "Any of you try to run out, I swear I'll hunt you down and kill you. You go along with me and we'll all get a cut."

With that Danny Damiani broke into a run. He had to dodge many loose rocks and larger boulders but finally reached Warlow. Warlow was still looking at him thoughtfully, wearing a puzzled frown.

Danny Damiani's gaze searched the whole slope as he moved anxiously about, kicking rubble out of the way and muttering to himself.

"Like I said, Damiani," Warlow told him. "There isn't any hole. Maybe there never was one."

Damiani shook his head, refusing to believe this. "I seen Torp Berry go down on his knees. O'Shea, too, and Shepherd. And Berry called out that he'd found the gold."

"Well, I ain't standing in the sun looking any longer, Damiani. If you want to, that's your business. Me, I'm seeking shade and I'm going to rest before I fall apart."

"Don't move," Damiani ordered him. He moved restlessly back and forth across the slope until he suddenly stopped beside a huge boulder. His eyes lit up and a smile broke onto his bruised mouth.

Then pointing to the side of the boulder, he said excitedly, "See that, Warlow. Somebody shifted it back in place. Got dirt on this side, the side which shouldn't ever have touched the ground. So you get those fools up here with bars and shift it away. We've got to the end of the trail, mister, and nobody's going to stop us from here."

Warlow went tiredly down the hill again and organized the prisoners with iron bars. He told Curly Bromage about the filled-in hole and Bromage looked curiously at May Soncum.

May held his stare for a long time before she asked hopefully, "Could it possibly be Mr. Durant, Mr. Bromage?"

"Who else could budge those rocks, ma'am?" Bromage said, smiling, and his gaze swung to take in the range beyond the slope.

"Where is he then?" she asked.

Bromage's smile remained fixed on his face. "Like he's proved often enough, Miss Soncum, Durant's a patient man. He don't take chances. When he does something, it comes off, and my guess is he's just biding his time now, waiting for the best moment to attack. I think I best get up near Danny so I can maybe help Durant out some."

"Be careful," May told him and Bromage looked at her as if seeing her for the first time. When she lowered her eyes, and color rose in her cheeks he mumbled something to himself. Then he struggled up the slope and stood just behind Danny Damiani.

Damiani gave him a curious look but when Bromage folded both hands about his middle and looked to be suffering, he returned his attention to Warlow and four helpers.

Warlow pulled back on the bar and urged the others to give it all they had. Slowly, inch by inch, the big rock rolled up, shook a little as its full weight went onto the iron bars then began to roll.

Warlow dropped his bar and jumped out of the way and Danny Damiani, after watching the rock gather speed, went down onto his knees on the rim of the wide, dark hole in the ground.

His eyes sparked with excitement as he peered down but the blackness of bare earth was all the reward he got. He rose, dusted his hands and knees and looked crazily about him.

Josh Warlow moved urgently away from him and Curly Bromage, stunned by the savagery in his former trail friend's face, said, "Take it easy now, Danny. Take it easy, man."

Damiani wheeled, bringing his gun to bear on him. An insane look of cunning burned now in his dark eyes. "Got it, Curly," he babbled. "Got it all, and for myself and nobody else. Now you get down there and line up those men. Ain't nobody going to get away from here to tell what happened."

"There's still Blake Durant," Bromage told him quietly.

Damiani frowned heavily. "He's gone."

"No," Bromage told him.

Damiani stuck the gun hard into Bromage's middle. "I said he's cut out, Curly. I seen him go."

Bromage shook his head and pointed to the hole. "Who else could have rolled that stone into place, Danny? Maybe me when I wasn't shot up. But nobody else and you know it. It would take a man of Durant's size and Durant's strength to do it and you know it."

Damiani went pale and shook his head desperately. "I seen him go," he said again, but then he looked anxiously about him. Curly Bromage moved away from him but even as he moved Damiani brought the gun to bear on him. "He's here then, Curly?" he asked wildly.

"I reckon so."

"Where then? Where, damn you?"

"I don't know, Danny. But he's close by. He got here first, rolled that stone back in place and he's waiting to see what you do from now on. Maybe he's got a gun."

"I do have a gun," came Blake Durant's voice from the top of the slope.

Bromage and Damiani both looked up to find him standing there with Torp Berry's body planted in front of him as a shield. Damiani jerked his gun up and without warning pumped off a shot.

Torp Berry let out a cry of pain as the bullet slammed into him, then went limp. Blake Durant tossed him idly aside and stood with feet planted wide.

He said dully, "That's your last bullet, Damiani. Might as well drop the gun."

Damiani punched the gun forward as his finger dug at the trigger. But Blake Durant's count proved to be correct.

He spared one last glance for the unmoving Torp Berry, then made his way down towards Danny Damiani.

Damiani lifted his hands and made fists of them, clearly not yet willing to admit defeat. Curly Bromage moved away from him, biting his lip, even now feeling sympathy for a man he had once liked a great deal.

Blake Durant came on steadily and Damiani backed off. Then Blake said, "Watch the hole, Damiani. You're too close to it."

Damiani sneered viciously at him and went back another step. But his bootheel did not make contact with anything. With a cry he lost his balance and fell backwards and disappeared from sight. Curly Bromage was first to reach the side of the hole and went down on his knees to peer down into what was now a gaping hole.

Blake Durant touched his shoulder and when Bromage looked up, he said, "He has no chance."

"But we've got to look. Hell, we can't leave him lying down there to suffocate, die slow, maybe hurt bad."

"I checked when I came up. Gilbert's charges exploded too deep. There's a cavern under there and soon this whole slope will collapse. As for gold, if it's there, nobody will ever get it."

Curly Bromage still knelt there. Warlow came up and made his own inspection but then went off and made up a brush torch. Holding it down into the hole he and four other men peered down. But although the torch lit up the edges of the hole the light could not penetrate down into the depths.

Warlow let the torch fall into the hole and standing, said, "Guess Durant's right. Means all this misery has been for nothing. How many men were killed here?"

Nobody answered him.

May Soncum came up the slope and stopped just in front of Blake Durant. There were tears in her eyes. But then Curly Bromage came up and laid a hand on her shoulder. May turned, startled, and Bromage looked past her at Durant. He then extended his hand.

"You'll be pushing on, Durant?" he asked.

Blake thought about that a moment then studied the tearful May again. "I hadn't made up my mind until now," he said. "But I have my horse and all trails are open again. You'll make it, Bromage?"

Curly Bromage smiled and glanced at May Soncum. "I reckon I might if I take a nurse along, Durant," he said.

Blake shook his hand and put up Torp Berry's gun. He looked off into the distance where towering peaks reached up to the clouded sky. The air became suddenly cooler and he sniffed and thought he could smell rain. Turning, he collected Sundown and swung up. When he rode back, he saw May standing on her own, looking puzzled.

Sensing the reason for her uncertainty, he said, "A man looks for a woman who loves him. Bromage has been doing his looking, too."

May shook her head. "But Hopgood and—"

"No," Blake cut her off. "None of that matters. Good luck."

May brushed the tears from her face. "You're a strange man, Mr. Durant," she said.

But even as she spoke Blake Durant was riding off, heading out on a trail to nowhere.

He rode, a lonely figure, into the sun.